From the files of the Free City Inquisitor's Office:

The Ripple in Space-Time

I0668451

S F Chapman

Striped
Cat
Press
www.stripedcatpress.com

The Ripple in Space-Time
by
S F Chapman
is also available
as a Kindle e-Book

Publicity for S F Chapman and
The Ripple in Space-Time
exclusively by JKS Communications:
Contact Marissa@JKSCommunications.com

Learn more about the author at www.SFChapman.com

The phrase "From the files of the Free City
Inquisitor's Office"
and
the pawing cat logo are trademarks of
Striped Cat Press.

Visit us at www.stripedcatpress.com

Cover by Anderson Solutions and Design
Anderson_solutions_design@yahoo.com

Striped Cat Press
First Paperback Edition, Second Printing:
February 2013

To John Nelson;
a fine craftsman,
an affable father-in-law
and a longtime supporter of my work.

Acknowledgements

As I write, and I spend hours at it nearly everyday, my huge former feral cat *Lucky* stretches out nearby to watch over the work. He is the lone witness to the long and slow process.

When the task of creating the novel is complete the big cat takes a nap and the manuscript is handed over to a bevy of humans who help me craft it into the book that you hold in your hands.

The first to lend a hand, of course, are my three stalwart editors: Clint, Tina and Mark. All are excellent writers in their own rights, avid readers of science fiction and wonderful friends. Without their exceptional efforts my many novels would not have been possible.

But a book travels much farther than the comparatively short trip from author to editors. A cover is produced and the interior is laid out. For *The Ripple in Space-Time* Clinton D. Anderson, a superb Graphics Designer in the San Francisco Bay Area, did the work for me.

No one would ever see the final product without months of persistent attention by Literary Publicists and I have the great fortune of working with the best in the business. The highly perceptive and especially personable founder of JKS Communications, Julie Schoerke, has guided my two novels to date through the labyrinth of traditional and new media with the goal of gathering the attention of discerning readers. I have also enjoyed the splendid efforts by JKS Communication's Managing Director Marissa DeCuir Curnutte, Senior Publicist Sami Jo Lien and especially good-natured Associate Publicist Grace Wright.

Thank you.

Introduction

Of all of my eight works to date, I most enjoyed writing *The Ripple in Space-Time*.

I played around with ideas and put together chapter summaries for the book about a year and a half ago. I visualized a dark and gritty Film Noir-like world with danger and scoundrels skulking around every corner. It would be an archetypically bad world with just a few good guys trying to save the day.

I imagined Humphrey Bogart or perhaps Bruce Willis as the aging male protagonist. Rutger Hauer or Edward G. Robinson would be the sociopathic super villain. The rest of the characters would fall into place as typical of the genre.

I discovered a collection of newspaper clipping from the mid 1800's that my great great grandfather had pasted into an old ledger book. The articles that he collected were filled with the florid language that was common in newspapers of the day. As I read through dozens of accounts of local scandals, odd natural phenomenon and criminal misdoings I began to appreciate the heavy-handed use of adverbs and adjectives. I scribbled a few gems on a scrap of paper: "rapacious raiders" in a report about the lingering threat of piracy, "citizens brooding over the most retched of all human undertakings" to describe a Civil War commemoration, and, one of my favorites, "With speeds climbing ever higher and a confusing hodgepodge of systems to measure that velocity still persisting from the earlier days..." denoting an attempt to standardize the maritime "Knot."

I decided to intersperse these often overwritten "official accounts" of what was happening as "News Items" to counterpoint what the reader had already discovered to be untrue.

Enjoy the book as it was intended; I wrote *The Ripple in Space-Time* as a tongue-in-cheek romp though serious matters.

A list of characters is included in the Appendix

1. News Item: Obituary

Dateline: 30th of May, 2445; Free City, Earth

The Academy of Quantum Physics announced this morning that the brilliant Nobel Prize winning researcher, Dr. Jana Bethany Fesai has died. It was reported today that Dr. Fesai was thought to be one of the many victims of the still unexplained destruction two days ago of the immense Lunar Ultra Energy Research Laboratory on the plains of the Sea of Crisis.

Dr. Fesai was 51 years old.

Jana Fesai was born in Buenos Aires on August 23, 2393. As with most noncloned offspring of wealthy parents, Ms Fesai enjoyed a pampered and indulgent upbringing in South America before moving to Free City at age 17.

Ms Fesai was an honor student at the prestigious School of Advanced Physics at Free City University where she graduated summa cum laude in 2416.

Dr Fesai was awarded a Nobel Prize in 2438 for her extraordinary pioneering work with Tauons and massive Quarks, most notably the creation of dozens of stable "Tauonic" elements, including the unimaginably dense Tau Iron atoms.

The Ripple In Space-Time

Lunar authorities suspect that rogue moon miners may have inadvertently pierced the Antimatter Containment structure buried deep below the lunar surface. The resulting antimatter annihilation obliterated the huge facility. Earth-bound Astronomers report that a colossal new crater now marks the location of the doomed laboratory. Lunar investigators have been unable to approach the site due to extremely high radiation levels.

The Warlord Syndicate, which has generously funded the Ultra Energy Laboratory and hoped to benefit greatly from the promising research conducted there, has asked the impartial Free City Inquisitor's Office to investigate the Lunar catastrophe.

The family of Dr. Fesai has yet to announce memorial plans.

2. The impartial inquiry

Xylitol?

What in the world is xylitol?

Ryo Trop refocused his flagging attention back to the top most sheet on the seemingly unending stack of Bills of Lading.

As a 54-year-old Investigator Second Class for the Free City Inquisitor's Office, he was obligated to find out how and why 27 kilograms of xylitol had gone missing.

He rubbed his weary eyes. The investigation into freight pilferage at the Municipal warehouse was into its third bleary week with little progress to show for the nearly one hundred hours of work.

Ryo slid his fingertips over his desktop interface screen and carefully pronounced the word, "Xylitol; definition and commodity price please."

The small shiny rectangle retrieved the required information, *"Xylitol is a crystalline artificial sweetener with qualities similar to common sugar. Current market price is 1.28*

Standard Units per kilogram. Chemical formula:
$CH_2OH(CHOH)_3CH_2OH$."

Ryo shook his head in annoyance. So a quantity of imitation sugar worth about as much as a good dinner for two had gone unaccountably astray? Over almost thirty-five years at the preeminent and highly regarded Free City Inquisitor's Office, he had developed a reputation for being very thorough and uncompromising when investigating sensitive or potentially embarrassing matters.

This investigation into the minor theft of nearly worthless commodities was a terrible waste of his talents, especially so close to his planned retirement in two years.

He set aside the suspect document for future scrutiny.

• • •

Lev Fesai stared at the photograph of his mother and tried to recall when he had last seen her in person. It was about four years ago, he realized, when she turned over the house to him just before leaving for the Ultra Energy Lab on the Moon.

Now she was dead.

The young man gently placed the smiling image of his mother back on to the side table.

Lev didn't feel like a 28-year-old orphan. He almost expected to receive a fresh video message from her at any time, she'd sent him five or ten second greetings several times a day for many years.

Lev dolefully played the final dispatch that had waited unviewed for the last two days.

"Lev, Something strange has happened here. Take care of my cat. Love, Ma." The message ended with a blurry frozen image of his mom staring off screen in distress.

Something wasn't quite right about this message; he watched it a second time.

The jerky video ran its course.

He stared at the final image of his mother, she still didn't seem to be gone for some reason; scared but not dead.

Perhaps he was trying to avoid the obvious, Lev realized.

Many people, including his Grad student advisors at the University Advanced Physics Department had browbeaten him recently about his deplorable lack of motivation and his aimless avoidance of responsibility. He just wasn't ready for the rigors of a science career like his mother's that involved a lamentable lack of uninhibited mirth and self-indulgence.

Oddly, he noted with a start, his current hedonism coincided with his mother's departure for the Moon.

The overly large home that they had shared for most of his life had suddenly became a sterile and inhospitable place without her. For weeks he moped around the empty townhouse. His mother had suggested from afar that he should find some roommates to fill the vacant bedrooms on the third floor and eventually Lev advertised for some renters.

A quirky art student named Desiree moved in a few weeks later and quickly set about repainting the unimaginative dwelling with elaborate murals. She was an amusing whirlwind of activity and entertainment; Lev particularly admired Desiree's propensity for enjoying the moment. She quickly recruited him into the developing Enlightenment Crusade, a somewhat subversive nonconformist movement at the University.

Before long, his house was filled of an ever-changing group of Enlightenment Crusaders.

Slowly he had let his tiresome obligations slip away in favor of the pleasure-seeking ways of his new lifestyle. The small amount of rent that he sporadically collected had kept him going for years without a regular job.

Now what? With his mother gone perhaps he should renew his efforts to eventually succeed her as the leading authority on Tau Hadrons and Ultra Energy Physics.

He played her final message again.

"Lev, Something strange has happened here. Take care of my cat. Love, Ma."

He studied the final frozen image of her for many minutes. Lev noticed an especially disturbing juxtaposition between the cheerful photo and the jarring message screen. It didn't make sense. The researchers at the lunar lab were absurdly cautious about the handling of the unstable antimatter that they produced in the giant well-protected reactors.

Perhaps he should contact the investigators with his concerns.

• • •

"Ryo, come into my office for a consultation."

He smiled pleasantly at small image of his ever-grumpy 68-year-old boss, "I'll be right there, Helga."

The screen faded. 'Consultation' nearly always meant that he'd soon have a new assignment. Ryo gleefully set aside the tedious shipping documents; hopefully any new work would take him out into the huge metropolis of Free City. A perplexing murder or complex case of racketeering could keep him out of the dreary office for months.

He strolled cheerily across the hallway.

Ryo pushed open the door. Helga was, as usual, hunched behind her ancient desk glowering at her desktop interface screen. Inspector Fourth Class Edwin Chin stood timidly off to the side. A striking young man with an unruly head of curly black hair and dressed in the outlandishly colorful fashions of the Enlightenment Crusade sat on the austere office chair facing his perpetually sour boss.

Helga began without formalities; "Mr. Chin has been fumbling about with this Lunar Lab disaster for two days now."

The novice detective cringed at the woman's displeasure.

"We've just come across some new evidence that will require the instincts of a more veteran staff member." Her eyes narrowed, "Chin, I'm switching you and Mr. Trop effective immediately. Head across the hall and finish up his work on the pilferage inquiry."

She pointed at the door and the hapless man shuffled off.

When the door slammed shut, Helga briefly smiled at Ryo, "This is Lev Fesai, son of the presumed dead Dr. Jana Fesai who, as I sure you are aware, was employed as the Chief Researcher at the recently destroyed Lunar Laboratory."

Ryo chuckled to himself, this was already much more interesting than tracking down a few missing kilos of artificial sweetener.

For the next hour, the young visitor recounted his growing suspicions about what had happened several days earlier at the complex on the plains of the Sea of Crisis.

Ryo pressed his fingertips against his furrowed brow, "Play the message again for me, Lev."

The lanky young man complied.

"Lev, Something strange has happened here. Take care of my cat. Love, Ma."

"You see, Mr. Trop..."

The older man held his hand up, "Lev, just call me Ryo."

"OK, Ryo," he bit his lip for several seconds, "if miners had accidentally ruptured the antimatter containment structure, as the press seems to think, there wouldn't have been any warning."

"I don't follow."

Lev tapped idly on the message screen. "My mom would have been killed in an almost instantaneous fireball before she could send off the dispatch."

Helga nodded sternly in agreement.

"Alright;" Ryo replied, "I'll get to work on this case right away."

"Before you leave, Mr. Trop," Helga glanced at the younger man, "I'd like you to include Lev in as much of the investigation as you see fit."

Lev stared at Ryo with a particularly pleading look.

Helga eyebrows arched up in anticipation.

Ryo sighed and scrawled out directions for Lev, "Meet me at this address at 9:30 tonight."

3. News Item:
Free City Bicentennial preparations

Dateline: 30th of May, 2445; Free City, Earth

Free City Mayor Lily Borja detailed the elaborate preparations pertaining to next year's Bicentennial celebrations for the fair city today.

At a daylong media conference in City Hall, Mayor Borja unveiled detailed renditions and models of the several pavilions sponsored by some of Free City's most prominent institutions and organizations.

The ornate exhibit submitted by the Free City Historical Society garnered much attention by the conference attendees. The group plans to reenact the long history of the autonomous and independent municipality from its origins more than two hundred and fifty years ago as a disorganized refugee camp on the northern edge of the Shannon Basin following the anarchy at the conclusion of the Second Amero-Asian War to its much revered current status as the sole shining light of freedom and enlightenment in the otherwise grim Solar System.

Free City University will highlight the many
achievements that have sprung from the
venerable institution in the last two centuries.
Foremost, of course, is the extensive effort to
store progressively higher energy densities in
ever-smaller spaces, mainly by developing
various pairings of matter and antimatter. The
work carried out at the recently destroyed Lunar
Ultra Energy Lab run by the University
undoubtedly will receive significant scrutiny by
the celebrants.

The Free City University Student Union is
organizing a colorful parade that will progress
through the city on most Saturdays during June
and July. The parade participants will include the
many social organizations that are currently
active at the institution. The largest contingent
will likely be the Enlightenment Crusaders with
adherents attending from the city and all seven of
the fiefdoms. The group has promised to
highlight its nonconformist and experimental
nature in lively and most likely noisy detail.

The Free City Municipal Government plans to
accentuate the city's unique position as the lone
bastion of impartiality in the sea of corruption
and inequity that pervades life outside the
metropolitan borders. To that end, both the High
Court and the Inquisitor's Office have produced
several documentaries about the ongoing efforts

to reduce graft and extortion amongst the seven quarrelsome leaders of the Warlord Syndicate.

The Warlord Syndicate for its part will promote the dozen or so vacation destinations in the seven fiefdoms beyond the borders of our fair city. It's hoped that the wealthier and more adventurous residents of Free City will endeavor to travel abroad to enjoy holidays in the fiefdoms. Current statistics reveal that city vacationers travel primarily to the venerable Sea of Tranquility Historical Resort on the Moon and the rugged Australian Outbacks Theme Park in IndoPacifica.

The Bicentennial Exposition will take place in Roscommon Park from March 16 to August 23, 2446.

4. Contacts and cohorts

Lev was waiting for him just outside of the particularly seamy *Club Glut* on Fourth Street.

Ryo shook his head in dismay at the two work-weary prostitutes halfheartedly hustling several well-dressed teenage boys in front of the raucous nightspot. The boys laughed nervously at the old hookers before slipping into the club.

"Have you been here before?" Lev shouted above the pounding beat that pulsed out of the open doors.

"I'm not a regular," Ryo grinned, "but I have been here far too often."

The young man advanced towards the ticket kiosk but the old Investigator waved him off. Ryo held up his Inquisitor's Office badge and the attendant nodded tepidly.

Just beyond the doors, the club was a sweaty and confusing mass of wannabe dancers, vibrantly attired Enlightenment Crusaders and inebriated office workers all gyrating to the painfully loud and pervasive beat.

Ryo tugged Lev towards the huge bar that stretched along one sidewall. While they waited for a bartender, several statuesque women nearby gawked at Lev.

Ryo chuckled; young love, or at least pheromones, were in the air.

Far down the long bar, the head bartender noticed the men.

"Ryo Trop, you old dog! What brings you here tonight?"

"Just catching up on a little work." He nodded to the bar man, "Hey Vayk, how's business tonight?"

"I can't complain and if I do, no one listens anyway. Do you two want anything?"

Ryo shook his head, "Nothing for me."

Lev smiled playfully, "I'll have a Gin and Tonic."

The bartender's bushy eyebrows arched up, "Oh, a traditionalist; hopefully I can find some gin here somewhere."

"Before you go off hunting for ancient spirits," Ryo's hand clasped the man's wrist, "I'm looking for a Mining Guild Appraiser named Thacker who's supposed to be here somewhere.

Have you seen him tonight?"

"Yeah, Mr. Thacker is in Rumpus Room 3 with a few of the local tarts."

"Excellent," Ryo waved his fingertips over the bartender's payment interface, "we'll take the drink in Room 3 then."

The small rectangular interface attached to the barman's bicep summarized the financial transaction, *"Ryo Trop, the premium well drink tab is 13 Standard Units. Do you wish to leave Mr. Vayk a tip?"*

He nodded to the hopeful bartender, "Yes, 50 Units for my most cooperative friend."

"Confirmed," the interface replied, *"63 Standard Units charged to Ryo Trop."*

The barman trotted off with a wide grin.

Ryo smirked curtly at the loitering women before he and Lev left the bar for the long and slow trip across the tumultuous dance floor to Rumpus Room 3.

A stocky guard blocked the door to the private room until Ryo's badge caused him to flinch away in panic.

Rumpus Room 3 was surprisingly quiet compared to the deafening hypnotic swirl of the dance floor, the room seemed much more like a softly lit parlor in a fine Free City house than a side area to the wild nightlife just outside.

Near the center of the opulent lounge, huddled around a large low table, sat a husky middle-aged man with three ridiculously thin and vacuous young women.

The man looked up in alarm at the intruders.

Ryo noticed a great deal of contraband aphrodisiacs and hallucinogens spread out on the table, "Mr. Thacker, I'm Investigator Trop from the Inquisitor's Office."

The women rustled nervously.

With so much illicit activity transpiring in this room, Ryo mirthfully noted, one way or another he'd easily get whatever information that he needed.

"Mr. Thacker, may I remind you that these items are prohibited in Free City." He tersely added, "Are these young ladies of legal age and registered with the Courtesan's Union?"

The big man shifted anxiously, "Well, I..."

"Fortunately for you," Ryo declared, "I'm not working with the Vice Detail tonight. However if things don't go well, I may have to call them in for a bit of advice."

The detective's power play caused two of the women to whimper uncontrollably.

The Mining Guild Appraiser was sweating profusely, "Mr. Trop, how may I assist you tonight?"

Ryo studied the big man for an uncomfortably long time before answering, "I have some questions about unsanctioned mining operations near the Lunar Ultra Energy Lab just before its destruction."

"Oh; that," Thacker sighed with relief.

• • •

Two hours later Ryo waved absently to Lev as the younger man boarded the city transport across the street from the club with one of Thacker's underage woman. The investigator withdrew the communication device from his pocket and waited several minutes in the brisk night air before he contacted his boss.

"Well," Ryo summarized, "the Mining Guild Appraiser says that there almost certainly wasn't any mineral extraction going on near the Lab before the blast."

The tiny image of Helga frowned on the communication display, "And you're confident that he's a reliable source?"

"Absolutely." Ryo nodded, "The Mining Guild is especially adept and draconian at detecting even the tiniest tunneling operations." He smiled at his stern supervisor; "They make billions every year in fees from both legitimate and illicit endeavors. Apparently they can even catch a single rouge miner with a hand spade and a rusty wheelbarrow."

His implacable boss didn't seem to be amused by his dry humor.

"Damn it," Helga muttered. "The mischievous miners run amuck theory would have neatly explained the catastrophe. Now we seem to have a much more nettlesome mystery, who or what really caused the explosion? With nearly all of the physical evidence destroyed or buried under tons of radioactive lunar rubble, it's going to be particularly difficult and time consuming to discover what happened."

"So what's next?" he asked.

For just a brief instant she looked very weary, "The heat is on in this matter, hundreds were killed and a very expensive facility was destroyed. The Warlord Syndicate is especially displeased that their huge investment was lost and there is a colossal amount of pressure being applied to the Inquisitor's Office to come up with some answers."

The steely old woman scowled, "We need to find the right answers, not some phony smokescreen. You're going to have to rummage around in the outside world, I'm afraid."

"Yeah, I figured as much." Ryo slumped in dismay, despite his keen desire to remain in the comparative safety of Free City, the investigation was already tugging him inextricability out into the unruly domain of the Warlords.

"Alright," Helga puffed, "you have a full expense account for this matter, but I expect some results that I can report to the press in the next few days. Ryo, because of the complexities of this case, I want you to work with a Fiefdom Liaison Agent."

"Mackillroy?" he asked hopefully.

"No, Mac's busy with the assassination in New Rome. I'm sending you the address of someone new, a promising young Liaison Agent named Norton who's currently tending to some trivial matters in Dublin."

The screen faded.

Dublin, Ryo winced, was a hazardous two-hour trip beyond the Free City limits and well into the lawless neighboring fiefdom of EurAfrica.

5. News Item:
The pirate scourge continues

Dateline: 3rd of June, 2445; Free City, Earth

The recent spat of space piracy and hijacking continues to vex transportation officials and ship owners.

Dozens of vessels, both large and small, have suffered the ill effects of the marauding raiders. Most small ships have been quickly set free upon payment of ransom demands but a few especially valuable large freighters are still being held as the criminals negotiate ever-larger payoffs.

The Warlord Syndicate, which has sustained significant losses at the hands of the thieves, announced that it would soon offer a bounty of up to ten thousand Standard Units each for several suspected outlaws.

Four ships remain inexplicability missing, most notably the notorious *Butin Belle* which disappeared near Mars almost three months ago. The infamous ship is a small, fast and highly maneuverable Ore-Runner Class midget space freighter used primarily in the past by illicit miners in the Asteroid Belt. The craft's

comparatively small size and great speed
allowed the former clandestine operators to
evade Mining Guild inspectors.

The *Butin Belle's* main engine is a ubiquitous
and very powerful ion drive that can propel the
craft to an impressive maximum speed of over
45 Astronomical Units per year.

The *Butin Belle* had been engaged recently by
Celestial Delivery Systems as a quick transporter
between Mars and the Kuiper Belt Station in the
Outer Reaches. Both Celestial Delivery Systems
and Warlord Syndicate Underwriters are eager to
recover the valuable and one of a kind vessel.

Anyone with information regarding hijacked
vessels or the activities of pirates should contact
the Free City Inquisitor's Office or the Vessel
Registry Bureau.

6. A call to action

Lev peeked into the clamorous Student Union meeting room.

Dozens of garishly dressed Enlightenment Crusaders roamed about the overfilled hall. Many haphazardly flitted between small clusters engaged in trivial conversations about recent shenanigans or solemn flocks conducting weighty discourses regarding lofty future goals.

More than a few of his self-indulgent companions were undoubtedly under the influence of herbal stimulants or mild hallucinogens, Lev mirthfully noted.

He'd vacillated for several days as to whether or not he should attend the much-publicized meeting; past gatherings of the Crusaders had lapsed into contentious shouting matches or medicinally induced mass debauchery.

Lev grinned at the hand drawn multicolored sign that someone had proudly posted at the door: *Crusade Brainstorm Today! Help us conceptualize the future of the Movement!*

The disjointed group certainly needed some direction, he reluctantly concluded.

He slipped into the noisy room.

"Lev!" a chubby teenage girl draggle-tailed up and hugged him. The elaborate rainbow beadwork on her loose fitting halter top rustled softly.

Although he vaguely recognized the overly affectionate youngster, he could not recall her name. Lev kissed the top of her grimy head, "Hey, how have you been?"

"Good, good!" She stared up at him with an unnerving sense of utter idolization. "Are you going to help us put together some virtuous goals for the future?"

Lev absently studied her jiggling breasts as she spoke; "I don't know about virtuous," he dryly added, "maybe just laudable and noteworthy."

The girl nodded with absurd sincerity at his quip. "Come join us!" She tugged him towards a loitering group of a dozen or so giggly teens.

She was Desiree's little sister, Lev realized belatedly; the plump teen was called Sadie or Sabra, something like that, she had almost certainly visited the house when Des lived with him.

The public address system screeched painfully.

The Ripple In Space-Time

"OK, we'd like to begin," a willowy redheaded woman said hopefully to the boisterous throng. "I know there aren't any chairs...but could everyone please sit down on the floor?"

Gradually the gathering of idiosyncratic individuals complied with the request.

Lev slipped away from his girlish admirer and found his way to an strangely mismatched flock of cheery wide-eyed street people, eccentric self-obsessed dilettantes and forward-thinking academics like himself.

"Thank you," the MC finally said with visible relief.

"Before we begin, I must remind everyone that University policy strictly forbids the use of unprescribed medications and herbal treatments in any of the school facilities."

Scattered boos echoed through the hall.

"For the first half of the morning session, we are most fortunate to have as a guest speaker Professor Malcolm Evans from the School of Biology."

During the tremendous applause that followed, the jaunty fortyish Professor waved wholeheartedly to the gathering.

"Good morning everyone!"

The applause began anew.

When the adoring group finally quieted, he continued, "Several years ago when the Enlightenment Crusade first coalesced in the School of Biology, it was just a group of five very imaginative students who wanted to change the way that things were done."

Loud cheering interrupted the speech.

"Those five innovators had no idea at the time that eventually the Crusade would have tens of thousands of enthusiasts in Free City and the seven fiefdoms."

Lev nodded along with many others at the recounting of the organization's rapid growth.

"However, I sometimes fear that the movement has lost its way; that the simple ideals of enlightenment, social justice and equality have been forgotten and replaced by less noble distractions."

The Professor pointed accusingly at the uneasily stirring audience.

"If we are to move forward, let's remember that self-indulgent thrill-seeking is not the same as experimentation to discover a greater enlightenment, that grumbling about the benign status quo is not the same as crying out for social justice, and that the commonplace advantages of the most fortunate must be equally shared with the underprivileged."

"YEAH!" a shaggy fellow yelled from the left side of the hall, "That's what it's all about people!"

The speaker smiled at the enthusiastic firebrand.

"There's a great deal of untapped energy in this room. Energy that could easily be squandered on a thousand trivial and uncoordinated projects or carefully focused on achieving a greater good for all."

Slowly the enthusiasm of the marshaled idealists built up.

A deafening fugue of inharmonious cheering filled the venue.

"EN...LIGHT...EN...MENT!" The approving roar of the crowd gradually evolved into a thunderous synchronized chat, "Enlightenment! Enlightenment!"

Nearly everyone was standing.

For several minutes the Professor beamed at the wholehearted demonstration.

"I would be most proud," he finally continued, "to discover in the near future that a great modern day crusade of the concerned had left the safety and opulence of our fair city and ventured out into the cruel injustice and servitude of the wider world to struggle for the freedom and dignity that all people deserve."

In a wide sweeping arc, the speaker pointed to everyone in the crowded hall, "YOU ARE THOSE PEOPLE!"

As Lev chanted along with the booming and euphoric multitude, he pleaded to himself that he would somehow be instrumental in improving the lives of all humankind.

7. The *Butin Belle*

Jana Fesai pensively studied the stars through the small porthole of her dreary little compartment.

The vessel would soon cross the orbit of Mars and now seemed destined for the rocky chaos of the Asteroid Belt; the perfect place to hide a shipload of hostages and a great deal of stolen materials.

She pushed off from the wall and drifted slowly across the tiny cell. Her captors apparently considered her a valuable commodity, while the other victims were locked away together elsewhere, Jana for some reason was the given the "privilege" of solitary confinement.

The isolation was closing in on her.

She'd been striving mightily for days to avoid the looming insanity that would be brought about by the prolonged solitude. Often she had wistfully daydreamed about Lev far away in the comfort and relative safety of Free City. Sometimes she had methodically reviewed every possible characteristic of each of the 92 natural elements on the Periodic Table or slowly recited Shakespeare's *A Midsummer Night's Dream* which she'd memorized as a high school Junior in Buenos Aires thirty-six years earlier.

But she could still feel the slow creeping tendrils of madness entwining her psyche.

Jana writhed suddenly in defiance of the desolation; somehow she would force herself to persevere.

She had no reasonable way of knowing how long it had been since she and the others had been snatched from the Ultra Energy Lab on the Moon.

Jana had struggled to find anything that seemed to occur with predictable regularity. She'd given up on trying to discern some sort of pattern from the sporadic mechanical sounds that pervaded the ship. Jana had tallied the dreadful rations that were delivered haphazardly by a vacant and begrimed black-haired boy; the count was now seven, of which she'd been willing to eat only two.

If they were feeding her twice a day, Jana reasoned, then she'd been taken prisoner about three days ago.

Her stomach growled in disagreement. Perhaps her meals were served only once a day, in which case she'd been locked in this tiny room for a week.

Reluctantly, Jana concluded, that seemed the more likely scenario.

The Ripple In Space-Time

• • •

"Try it again, you bonehead," Captain Olin Gristle wearily told his First Mate.

"Fine!" Bosco Kremerling slammed the metal cover shut on the back of the communication console, "But I'm not talking to the bastard if we do manage to fix it."

Olin rolled his eyes, Bosco was particularly short tempered even for a pirate.

Perhaps reason would work with his testy subordinate, "Look Boz, we're never gonna get paid off for this little crime spree unless we finish things up the way that he wants them."

Bosco adjusted the output controls and reset the frequency. "You talk to him then," the belligerent second in command of the recently expropriated *Butin Belle* balled his fists in displeasure, "Given the chance, I'm likely to slit his throat or ram this ship into his friggin' living room."

"Alright, I'll talk to him."

It had been over a week since the band of seven pirates had snuck into the Moon base and made off with five prisoners and much more loot than they had expected. Their employer had asked for only one particular man and woman who were locked up separately in two of the ship's cargo holds and about five kilos of the weird antimatter iron that they made at the lab. He and Boz planned to ransom the others and sell off the rest of the valuable stolen materials.

And of course the device, Olin grinned. The heavy little sphere that they had nabbed from the Lab was the centerpiece of the whole scheme.

They were supposed to contact their employer three days ago, but the communication system was on the fritz. The Captain bit his lip and began his much-delayed message, "This is bluebird calling big boy. We have your birthday presents and the guests of honor. We're awaiting your invitation to the party." He pressed the send button.

Due to the huge distance that the message would travel, they wouldn't receive a reply for at least two hours.

The First Mate had a sour look of contempt as he watched the Captain send off the cryptic dispatch.

"I'm gonna look in on our precious passengers," Bosco finally muttered as he drifted out of the control room.

• • •

"Indium, Atomic Number 49. A very soft silvery-white post-transition metal," Jana whispered to herself, "Symbol: In. Atomic Weight: 114.818. Eighty-six known isotopes, two of which are stable."

She grinned waggishly, "One of the 'stable' isotopes is mildly radioactive."

"Tin, Atomic Number 50...."

A distant clatter interrupted her solitary discourse.

Jana stiffened in dread; someone was coming.

The cover over the small rectangular window on the door slid open, two disquieting dark eyes scrutinized her for nearly a minute. Finally the bolt of the heavy hatch disengaged and the thick metal door opened.

It was one of her capturers, Jana surmised uneasily.

A glowering and scraggily brute propelled himself into the chamber. His forward momentum slammed them both against the cold outer wall. The intruder clamped his big hands around her waist.

Jana stared at him in terror. His odor was

34

hideous, like a sickening combination of carrion and rubbish bins.

The hoodlum growled, "I would have porked you days ago."

He drew out a long, thin and very sharp dagger from a well-worn sheath dangling from his hip.

The thug's rough hand tightened around the knurled black handle as he brought it slowly and menacingly towards Jana's neck.

"You're too damn old and ugly to sell off to the Sex Slavers," he snarled.

The point of the grimy blade traced the line of her jawbone.

Jana could feel her skin part under the tip. The warm wetness of fresh blood trickled out.

She clinched her eyes closed in horror.

Surely he meant to kill her.

The beast cackled at her squeamishness.

He finally shoved her away in disgust, "Luckily for you, the Captain says that you're most valuable to us in unmolested condition."

Jana opened her eyes.

He returned the now blood-streaked dagger to the sheath and sneered lasciviously at her, "Our employer requires your services as a forced laborer."

She stared at him in disbelief, "Forced labor for what?"

Jana wasn't entirely sure that she wanted to hear the answer.

The big man twisted Jana's wrists painfully behind her back and dragged her out of the cell, "Something to do with strange stuff that you made on the Moon."

• • •

Olin Gristle listened to the scathing message from his employer. He realized with some remorse that their current predicament was largely due to his First Mate's propensity for destruction.

He could hear Boz rattling down the passageway now. The big man was the only one of the seven pirates on board the *Butin Belle* that didn't traverse the ship in cat-like silence. Even the clumsy and dull-witted cabin boy could carry out his activities without making a sound.

Bosco blustered into the control room dragging

one of their indispensable hostages.

The Captain scowled, "What the hell are you doing with her?"

The First Mate grinned contemptuously, "Just taking the bitch around for a little tour of our splendid ship."

The woman seemed to be horrified and, except for a thin bloody gash on her jaw, unharmed.

"Stop fooling around," Olin glared at him, "we got a reply from the boss."

He played the message again, "*You idiots! You busted up the candy store when you collected the guests and presents. Now the shop owner is on the prowl with the watchdog. The party has been moved to the winter house. Get the package ready for Air Mail delivery. DON'T drive off the road again, you morons!*"

"Well, he seems a little pissed off," Boz smirked, "I guess my work is done."

Olin frowned, "I'm still trying to figure out the message." He doodled on a scrap of grimy paper, "I know where the winter house is and I've adjusted our course to get us there."

He stared at the prisoner for several seconds

before smiling, "I don't believe that we've been properly introduced; I am Captain Olin Gristle, currently the Master of the *Butin Belle*."

He bowed with an absurdly overdone flourish.

"And you are..?"

"Dr. Jana Fesai," she forced an uneasy smile.

Olin continued, "So nice to meet you, Dr. Fesai. Since I was tending to matters on board the ship at the time, I was unable to visit the Ultra Energy Lab when my First Mate and the rest of the crew arranged for you to join us."

She realized that the man was apparently fishing around for something.

"I understand that the Laboratory was quite impressive. Who paid the bills for all of the fine work that went on over there?" he tipped his head expectantly.

"The lab is run by Free City University, but the Warlord Syndicate funds the research."

The Captain winced, "I was afraid of that. So the Syndicate and probably the Free City Inquisitor's Office are poking around."

Good, Jana thought vindictively, now these

marauders were feeling a little pain.

"Boz, I told you that the explosion was too big! We were only supposed to cover our tracks, not destroy the entire complex."

"The Lab is gone?" Jana stared at the Captain in horror.

"Yes, I afraid so," Olin frowned at his First Mate, "Mr. Kremerling decided to detonate two kilos of antimatter, not the ten grams that I gave him for the job."

"Hey, I love fireworks," Boz shrugged.

Jana quivered at the revelation; the nearly three hundred people who worked at the lab had certainly been killed by the brazen stupidity of these criminals and their still unknown overseer.

The two pirates argued amongst themselves.

Although she too was likely doomed, Jana resolved to somehow resist the efforts of the thugs that now surrounded her. Just as her ancient ancestors had done in Poland during World War II, she would secretly and subtly sabotage her captors' ambitions.

8. Beyond the city limits

It was miserably early on a dreadful morning.

Ryo frowned disapprovingly as he stared out of the city transport while it plodded through the overcast metropolis.

He certainly didn't want a sidekick, especially someone so young and inexperienced in the complexities of investigative work, but he was beginning to feel a growing affinity for Lev Fesai that he didn't completely understand.

The man had just lost his mother, Ryo reflected, but there seemed to be more to the developing camaraderie than mere pity. They'd worked surprisingly well together the other night at *Club Glut*.

Lev seemed to be Ryo's exact opposite. He apparently had no difficulty understanding the obscure intricacies of advanced Physics with its many axioms and absolutes. But he was also surprisingly dedicated to the unrestrained and nonconformist lifestyle of the Enlightenment Crusade.

Ryo had always strived to be moderate in his views and deeds, a quality that had served him well for nearly 35 years as an Investigator. His restrained centrism no doubt trailed back to his long dead Taoist ancestors.

Perhaps he just enjoyed the young man's company in a paternal way. Ryo cringed at the sudden insight; it made him feel especially old.

He sighed ruefully; apparently his subconscious was hinting that he should end his decades long dithering and get on with cultivating a descendant.

The transport jittered to a stop at the ever-busy Breton Street. Ryo followed the dreary hourly workers out of the hulking vehicle and on to the blustery thoroughfare.

He apathetically studied the unfamiliar district. Hopefully he'd be able to locate his new cohort's residence in the confusing Old World layout that pervaded this side of the city.

After a protracted search that involved walking up and down the block several times, Ryo selected the ornate townhouse that he believed was most likely to be Lev's residence. He ascended the broad stairway and studied the wide front porch.

A burly gray tabby cat watched him suspiciously through the glass of the prodigious front window. It might well have been the animal that

The Ripple In Space-Time

Jana Fesai had worried about in her final message to her son, Ryo noted.

He knocked tentatively on the huge white door. The cat sprang away in alarm at the commotion.

The door opened.

"Oh, Ryo. Come on in," Lev mumbled lethargically.

The big cat warily watched the visitor from the far end of the entryway.

"I just got up," the younger man squinted out at the gloomy weather, "Do you want anything to eat or drink?"

"Well, what do you have?"

"Ah, I think we have some leftover bagels and somebody's just made coffee."

"Coffee?" Ryo could not believe his luck, "Where on earth did you get coffee?"

"It's not illegal is it?" Lev shuddered.

Ryo laughed, "No, it's just so rare now. I haven't had any since the Warlord Syndicate jacked up the duties on coffee beans and the Free City authorities retaliated by piling on exorbitant tariffs. I can't afford 250 Units for a cup of the precious stuff."

"Well, we've have plenty," Lev led him into the well-appointed kitchen, "just don't ask how we got it."

A rotund dark-haired woman wrapped loosely in a colorful blanket and nothing else smiled at Ryo from the cluttered dining table.

"This is Cyndi, she's one of my roommates. Cyn, this is Ryo Trop; he and I are going over to Dublin today."

Cyndi extended her hand in greeting, causing the blanket to cascade off of her bare right shoulder. "Are you the cop?"

Ryo shook her hand and studied the now exposed woman, "Not a cop; Investigator Second Class for the Free City Inquisitor's Office."

"OH."

Lev filled three white porcelain mugs with wafting black liquid, "Sugar?"

Ryo chuckled, "Sure, as long as it's not xylitol."

Both Lev and Cyndi stared at him in confusion.

"Yeah, sugar would be fine."

• • •

The two men bounced along in the transport towards the City Limits Check Point.

"Cyndi seems nice. Are you two an item?"

"Well;" Lev vacillated, "we do sleep together occasionally. But the Enlightenment Crusade is all about experimentation so I also pretty much bed down with everyone else in the house too."

"How very modern of you."

The transport groaned to a stop at the heavily barricaded Check Point. Dozens of weapons-toting Free City Militiaman watched vigilantly over the border crossing for unauthorized intruders from beyond.

Ryo and Lev joined the small group seeking to leave the civilized enclave.

A surly EurAfrican border guard summoned them through the gate, "Your names?"

"Ryo Trop and Lev Fesai."

"What is the nature of your activities in the Supreme Imperial Fiefdom of EurAfrica?" he growled at the two men.

Ryo rolled his eyes at the pretentious sentry,

"Free City Inquisitor's Case Number 2445-11057."

"Trop and Fesai," the border guard sneered at his interface screen, " you are free to enter EurAfrica."

They strolled past the Check Point.

Lev looked back at the dour sentinel, "I thought that you had to bribe the Fiefdom officials to get though the gate."

"The job has its privileges," Ryo smiled.

They filed past a long snaking line of destitute refugees undoubtedly all far too optimistic about their chances of entering Free City. Lev briefly studied two mucky teenage girls in the middle of the throng before offering them the remnants of a stale bagel that he had retrieved from his coat pocket.

"We need to get some ground transportation," Ryo craned his neck. "Hopefully we can find something, there aren't any trains or street transports on this side of the border."

He scowled at the dreadful conditions of the shantytown. "Years ago, I was able to hire a vehicle for a day or two but apparently most people never returned the jalopies when the lease was up. We may end up having to buy something for the trip."

They dodged past dozens of street vendors selling contraband and worthless doodads.

"Ah, here we go," Ryo grinned.

A garishly outfitted mud lot loudly proclaimed *Mwizi's Motor Vehicles*.

Ryo strolled past the entryway befouled with dozens of glittery mismatched flags. Lev cautiously followed.

The men tentatively examined several beat-up clunkers. Ryo beckoned to the lot attendant slumped apathetically in front of a tiny interface display. The man eventually approached the two potential customers.

"What do you guys want today?"

Ryo smiled superficially, "Do you rent vehicles for the day?"

"You're kidding, right?" The salesman shook his head sarcastically, "Outright sales only."

"Alright then," Ryo's eyes narrowed in annoyance, "we'd like to buy a three or four seat cruiser."

The attendant surveyed the dozen or so vehicles strewn around the lot. "What level of Antipersonnel Protection are we talking about here?"

Ryo rubbed his forehead in dismay; long ago personal transportation in the domain of the Warlords had reverted from the cozy mass friendliness of public transit back to the antisocial safety of traveling alone wrapped in a hulking cocoon of energy-wasting steel.

"It's been awhile since I've done this, remind me of the Protection options," Ryo was certain that final price that he would end up paying was quickly climbing in the salesman's mind.

A sardonic grin stretched across the man's face, "Well, you've got your Level One Protection which will stop rocks and small weapon's fire. But Level One would only be effective in your nicer neighborhoods of Free City if they still allowed personal transports in that prissy little fairyland."

Ryo impatiently cut the man off. "We're not going to keep the heap for more than a day. What do you recommend for a quick trip to Dublin?"

"Dublin's a rough place, I'd go with Level Eight Protection. That will stop all common weapon's fire and most types of explosives. If you were traveling at night, I'd insist on Level Ten."

"Naturally."

Forty-five minutes later, Ryo navigated a hulking rustbucket off the lot and down the pothole-pocked road toward Dublin.

• • •

Twenty minutes into the trip Lev was jolted out of an uneasy catnap by an outburst of weapon's fire. The unseen assailants caused no damage to the heavily fortified conveyance; Ryo didn't even bother to take his eyes off of the road during the halfhearted ambush.

The young man stared in lingering panic out the window of the creaky vehicle.

"Tell me about your mother," Ryo asked idly.

Lev contemplated the old Investigator for several seconds as he drew his attention back to the tedious road trip. "My mother," his shoulders slumped, "was my best friend for most of my life."

"Did you have a dad?"

"No;" he shook his head, "mom was too busy to go through all of that; I was the result of random insemination at the fertility clinic."

Lev tilted his head in curiosity, "What about you?"

48

"Cloned."

"I would have never guessed."

Ryo chuckled, "Not all clones are janitors and day laborers. Some of us managed to struggle our way up to Investigator Second Class."

"Did you...," Lev paused to consider the propriety of his question, "did you have anyone to raise you?"

"I was supposed to," Ryo sighed. "I'm a clone of my father who was a rural bribe collector for the Fiefdom of EurAfrica." The old Investigator winced, "When I was about four years old, he was killed by the side of the road by some highwayman."

The travelers jostled along in uneasy silence.

"Fortunately the neighbors sent me to the Institution for the Furtherance of Clones in Free City." He laughed, "Evidently they thought I was too cute to end up in the local EurAfrican orphanage."

"Well that was lucky for you," Lev nodded. "I know those fiefdom workhouses are pretty much the same as slave mills."

"It's not much better in Free City, I'm afraid," Ryo said.

"Really?"

The old Investigator smiled at his naive cohort, "You had someone who looked after you day and night for most of you life, right?"

Lev nodded.

"It's not that way for most clones, especially in institutions. Seven kids died in my ward during the first five years that I was at the Institution. Four from illness, one from suicide and two were beaten to death."

"I had no idea that it was so rough."

"Most people think that the cruel world stops at the city limits," Ryo shook his head in disappointment, "that everything is so much better in Free City compared to the fiefdoms. But it's not true. If it was, I'd be out of a job."

Lev considered the dismal assessment. "How did you end up at the Inquisitor's Office?"

Ryo smiled nostalgically, "Two things worked out just right; when I was eighteen, I started working at the Institution's accounting office. It was dreadfully dull but it did keep me busy. Just by chance, a minor embezzlement scandal caught the attention of the Inquisitor's Office and they sent over a young Investigator Third Class named Helga Bennet."

"Your boss?"

Ryo nodded, "She and I worked together for hours and eventually straightened out the mess. Helga liked my work and recommended me to the Recruiting Office. Within a year I was a Cadet Investigator."

"What was the second thing?"

He grinned wryly, "With my tough upbringing, I can spot trouble brewing long before anyone else."

• • •

Ryo decided that the two-hour road trip had been fairly uneventful as he steered the monstrous road machine through the citadel gates of Dublin. He paid their entry fees and the Dublin Municipal toll-taker directed them to the Free City Consular's house.

He pulled the creaky behemoth into an open space in front of the official resident. A brawny security guard barked loudly at them until Ryo presented his badge.

The guard bowed slightly in deference, "Sorry Inspector Trop, the locals are constantly trying to snatch this prized real estate."

"It's not a problem. Is Liaison Agent Norton inside?"

"Yes sir, Norton's been waiting for you."

Lev gawked at the fortress-like row house, "It seems so intimidating for a diplomatic building, almost like it was built to withstand a siege."

"Sadly, I think it was," Ryo noted.

The guard led them up the wide stairway and slid his fingertips over a small interface screen on the doorjamb. "Inspector Trop and his associate for Agent Norton."

After several seconds, the heavy steel door opened. A startlingly attractive young woman, probably in her mid-twenties, clad in stained blue coveralls and clenching an antiquated toilet plunger studied the visitors keenly. "Good morning gentleman, please come in and wait in the parlor for a few minutes. We're all attending to a regrettable household emergency with the old plumbing right now."

"Certainly," Ryo nodded to the reluctant plumber.

Lev scrutinized the fetching mahogany-haired woman as she hurried off to deal with the calamity. "I certainly wouldn't mind being on the household staff with her," he whispered.

9. News Item:
A somber Commemoration Day

Dateline: 9th of June, 2445; Roscommon Park, Free City, Earth

Residents solemnly observed Commemoration Day during several somber memorial events throughout the city yesterday.

The grim annual observance marks the end of the Second Amero-Asian War two hundred and forty-nine years ago and commemorates the loss of so many lives.

Most citizens stood in brooding silence at 11:18 AM to contemplate the most retched of all human undertakings. Nearly a million people endured a cold drizzle in Roscommon Park to lay symbolic notes to the dead at the War Atrocities Monument.

The destruction brought about by the Second Amero-Asian War is now widely regarded by scholars as on a par with, if not more detrimental to the advancement of human achievements than the slow and moldering decay of the earlier Dark Ages.

The Ripple In Space-Time

Many of the forbidden weapons from earlier conflicts were employed during the war with horrific efficiency. Biological agents, toxic gases, nuclear and high-energy particle weapons rendered Europe east of the Urals along with nearly all of Asia and North America poisoned and uninhabitable. By 2196 nearly 5 billion humans had fallen victim to the protracted conflict and its ghastly side effects.

All citizens of Free City are familiar with the savagery that obliterated the great cities of New York, Beijing, Moscow and many others; regrettably only a few of these ancient communities have been rebuilt, most notably New Rome. Nearly everyone has personally witnessed the persistent effects brought about by the cataclysm beyond Free City's borders in the domain of the Warlords.

The war had no winners and not a single armistice or peace treaty was ever penned by the battling nations. Indeed, the combatants had managed to not only slaughter their enemies, but also themselves. No mere piece of paper could be held high as a symbol of victory after the long and unforgivable folly.

10. The accomplice

Ryo and Lev had been waiting for twenty
anxious minutes in the parlor of the Free City
Consular's residence in Dublin as the house staff
noisily battled an especially tenacious plumbing
problem involving the third floor commode.
Loud thuds and profuse swearing sporadically
pervaded the official household. Through the
open sitting room door, the men watched a
worried old butler hobble by several times with
yet another thick stack of white bath towels to
sop up the gushing muck.

Finally the young woman who had met them at
the front door returned wearing clean khaki pants
and a heavy brown traveling coat.

"Thank you for waiting," she held her hand out
in greeting, "I'm Agent Keira Norton of the Free
City Fiefdom Liaison Office."

The alluring woman shook the men's hands.

"I...well...hello," Lev stammered giddily.

"I'm Inspector Trop," Ryo chuckled at the
younger man's reaction, "I believe that Mr. Fesai

is relieved that you are not an overweight middle-aged gent."

Agent Norton glared at the shaggy tongue-tied man, "This is Dr. Fesai's son? I read through the case files last night, but I had no idea that we'd be working with family members." She studied his quirky and unconventional clothing, "There was some mention of Mr. Fesai's baffling fascination with the Enlightenment Crusade."

Ryo's communication device chirped softly, "Hi Boss, what's up?"

"Have you located Agent Norton?" Helga inquired.

"Yeah, we just found her at the Consular's residence."

"Good," his irritable supervisor continued, "O'Neal in Bank Fraud just discovered a large and suspicious transaction that is undoubtedly a payoff of some sort."

"What does this have to do with the moon lab?"

Helga rubbed her forehead wearily, "The recipient was just let go as a Lunar Orbit Traffic Controller. He was on duty during the explosion."

"Interesting."

"He just charged several drinks in a Dublin bar,

I'm sending you the particulars."

The image of Helga changed to flashing text. Ryo studied the information for several seconds.

"Well; we'll get right to it, I suppose." He showed the address to Agent Norton, "Do you know where this place is?"

She nodded in dismay.

Keira winced, "I'm afraid that's not one of Dublin's finer districts."

Ryo tugged at Lev as he absentmindedly ogled their new colleague, "We have transportation, let's head over there now. How is it that you were unstopping the Consular's commode, Ms Norton?"

She smiled proudly to the old Investigator, "Well, as a Fiefdom Liaison, I've been procuring and screening new household staff members for the last few weeks. The Consular is quite particular about the credentials of his domestic employees. My guest room is upstairs right next to the misbehaving facilities."

Keira pulled open the front door and led the men out, "I plunged out the toilet twice on my first day here and the Consular fell in love with me."

"How did you pick up such a strange old skill?" Lev wondered as the threesome stood on the front porch. "Everyone in Free City uses waterless waste disposal, I don't think I've ever seen anything else."

Keira scowled briefly at Lev, "My parents ran Leitrim Imports in Free City when I was a kid and we were always moving around in the fiefdoms in search of new products. I've been to Mars twice and I lived in Dublin for several years."

"When difficulties present themselves," she shivered fleetingly before buttoning up her jacket against the chilly wind, "you learn really quickly how to deal with the copious crap in the fiefdoms."

• • •

Relegated to the tattered rear section of the lumbering old vehicle, Keira studied the two men in the only slightly more favorable front seats.

Ryo Trop was well known and highly admired by the staff of the Liaison Office. Keira considered herself especially lucky to be included in the particularly high profile case with such a respected Investigator. Certainly a favorable outcome to the inquiry would greatly enhance her prospects at the Liaison Office.

Although she had reservations about working with someone as inexperienced in investigative work as Lev Fesai, she was inexplicably interested in him. She studied him carefully as he gawked at the dilapidated neighborhoods of Dublin. He had an extraordinary headful of wayward black curls, far longer and less tidy than convention currently allowed. His smooth and fluid movements contrasted with his stark and angular features; not unlike a shark or a fast Interceptor spacecraft, she mused.

His brief dossier had mentioned his stalled efforts at obtaining a Doctorate Degree, minor use of herbal hallucinogens and his regrettable tendency towards womanizing; definitely not traits that Keira condoned, but there was some intriguing quality about him that she couldn't quite rationalize.

"How are you doing back there?" Ryo glanced in the rearview mirror.

Keira smiled at the fatherly Investigator, "I'm doing OK." She shifted around and leaned forward, "I've got a background question about the investigation. I'm afraid I don't know much about antimatter. I recall from High School that it has something to do with energy storage, but that's about it."

The Ripple In Space-Time

"You're asking the wrong guy," Ryo laughed.

"Fortunately we have one of the leading authorities on such things right here with us."

He nudged the preoccupied younger man.

"Antimatter; OK, let me see if I can explain it." Lev stroked his chin for several seconds. "Every subatomic particle with mass, and there are dozens, has an essentially identical opposite called an anti-particle. It's almost like a mirror image, I guess."

Both Ryo and Keira nodded.

"Electrons have an opposite called anti-electrons," Lev continued, "a few people still call them positrons. Electrons and anti-electrons have reversed electrical charges; negative for electrons and positive for anti-electrons. If they happen to encounter each other, annihilation occurs and they are completely destroyed, converting all of the mass of the two particles into energy in the form of gamma rays."

Keira frowned, "What does that have to do with energy storage?"

Lev smiled, "Since well before the Second Amero-Asian War nearly all energy storage has used antimatter. But there have always been
60

some big problems with handling antimatter. Mainly because storing a bunch of charged

anti-particles is particularly difficult."

Ryo glanced at Lev as he negotiated the potholed streets, "Why is that?"

"It's hard enough to keep the little beasties in a vacuum container completely devoid of even the merest trace of ordinary matter; anti-electrons all have the same electrical charge, so they repeal each other. That and the electrical attraction of the surface electrons on the inside of the container pull the anti-electrons to the walls of the container and annihilation occurs."

"So a vacuum bottle filled with antimatter will explode?" Keira asked in horror.

"It could," Lev chuckled, "but there's a clever trick that keeps that from happening."

"What?" Keira wondered.

"Magnets, or at least magnetic fields," Lev smiled. "About four hundred years ago, scientists produced anti-hydrogen for the first time, slowly over many years other anti-atoms were fabricated. All were fairly difficult to store until anti-iron was created. It could easily be indefinitely suspended in a vacuum container using magnets. The same magnets are used to manipulate the anti-iron into a reaction vessel where it is methodically pelted with single

regular iron atoms to cause the release of well-controlled amounts of energy."

Lev swiveled around to face her, "Now everything from electrical power plants to space freighters uses some sort of antimatter-based power system."

• • •

The cross-town trip had taken nearly an hour.

"Force will be necessary here," Keira warned Ryo, "probably blackmail as well," she added.

Her eyebrows arched up as she pointed surreptitiously to Lev while he stared out at the ramshackle neighborhood.

"Don't worry," Ryo snorted as he parked the hulking conveyance in front of the rundown pub, "we can take care of ourselves."

"I *do* have the Dublin Coroner on speed-dial," Keira quipped.

"That won't be needed."

"Before we get started here," he admonished his young cohorts, "I want to forewarn you both that no one will be leaving this pigsty in a body bag today."

Lev shifted uneasily at the caution.

Keira bit her lip and nodded.

"When we go in, I want Lev to wait quietly in the background." He stared sternly at the young man, "Keep an eye out for surprise attacks and for anyone trying to sneak out. Yell like hell if either happens."

"OK."

"Keira, I'll do the talking when we get inside, you stay well behind me and keep an eye out for trouble. This joker's not likely to want to cooperate."

Ryo took a deep breath and steeled himself for the coming confrontation, "Keira, will you alert the local beat cops that we may have some trouble here within the next half an hour? Tell them we'll call if we need help, otherwise they should stay away."

She quickly sent off the message as Ryo finished up his instructions.

The trio stopped on the sidewalk to study the battered exterior of the shady drinking establishment. A rusty marquee loudly proclaimed *Satan's Lair* in flashing red lights.

The Ripple In Space-Time

Just inside the door, Ryo stopped his cohorts for several tense seconds as his eyes adjusted to the gloomy tavern. A hideous and hefty bar woman scrutinized them from behind the counter. Several solitary late morning inebriates were scattered about at the booths and card tables.

Just as he had instructed them, his colleges took their positions.

Ryo watched the proprietor carefully as he approached the bar.

She flexed her heavily tattooed biceps menacingly, "You three don't belong here."

He produced his badge and her eyes narrowed, "I have information that an unemployed Traffic Controller named Julian Korbus is currently in this establishment."

She glanced involuntarily to the right.

"I want you to point him out to me and we'll escort Mr. Korbus out of here without any trouble."

The bartender shook her head contemptuously, "You Free City jerks don't have no authority in this town."

Ryo gripped the bar and lunged towards her

threateningly, "We're after the thugs who blew up that laboratory on the moon!" He sneered with seething rage, "Do you want to join them in a Syndicate prison?"

"HEY YOU BARFLIES!" the big woman shouted suddenly, "Has anyone seen Jules Korbus?"

Ryo didn't bother to turn around, he was certain that outburst was meant as a warning to one of the half dozen patrons in the dingy pub.

"I'll shut down this place if I don't find this idiot in the next two minutes," the old Investigator snarled.

"You've got no cause; my license and Municipal bribes are all paid up."

He slammed his fist hard on the greasy bar, "WE SHALL SEE!"

The commotion was too much for a sleazy looking fellow in a back booth, the man bolted for the side exit in alarm.

"RYO!" Lev bellowed.

Keira leapt sideways and grabbed the fugitive's arm, but he deflected her with a walloping gut punch that sent the woman crashing into a rickety table.

Ryo sprinted towards the escaping man but Lev got there first. The younger man tackled the escapee and the two tussled wildly on the filthy floor.

The old Investigator joined the fray. He got kicked hard in the left side and stumbled backwards, slamming his shoulder painfully against the unforgiving wall.

Lev jerked the bucking criminal to his feet and Ryo sprang forward and wrapped his arm around the man's neck.

"STOP!" Ryo tightened his python-like grip on the fugitive, "Stop or I'll snap your friggin' neck!"

The criminal's face grew red with asphyxia before he drooped limply and slumped to the floor.

A half an hour later, two leery young beat cops led the battered and bruised Julian Korbus out of the wreaked bar in handcuffs.

"Is there anything else before we go, Inspector?" the Sergeant asked.

Ryo stared angrily at the tattooed barkeeper standing defiantly behind the bar, "Yeah, shutdown this dump and lock up the bartender for impeding a felony investigation."

"It won't do much good, I'm sorry to say," the officer shook his head, "she'll be serving swill here again by Happy Hour."

"I'm counting on that," Ryo rubbed his aching shoulder, "hopefully the word will get out that the Inquisitor's Office isn't screwing around in this matter."

• • •

Hours later, after finally getting through to Free City, Ryo recounted the interrogation at the Dublin Lockup to Helga.

"You were right, Boss," a dull throbbing headache reminded him of the harrowing day, "Mr. Korbus just received ten thousand Units from two pirates as a payoff for destroying the lunar orbit traffic records for the day of the blast."

"Pirates?" Helga stared broodingly at him from the screen. "Why would pirates risk capture to wipe out some routine administrative records? I'll have Jackson check on the traffic data in the morning. Were the Dublin Authorities able to extract the names of the guys?"

"Yes," Ryo was still uneasy about the grilling techniques used by the locals, "Olin Gristle and Bosco Kremerling. Apparently Korbus was

cellmates with Kremerling in the Outer Reaches Penitentiary. I have no idea about Gristle."

"OK, I expect you and your two assistants back here sometime tomorrow."

11. News Item:
Bold hijacking near Saturn

*Dateline: 11th of June, 2445; Io Research
Station, The Asteroid Belt and Jupiter Colonies*

Reports continue to filter in to the Io Research
Station about the unprecedented and bold
hijacking of the immense robotic space tanker
Xenon Lightning 54 as it crossed the orbit of
Saturn en route to the huge Kuiper Gas
Refinement Facility yesterday.

Refinement Facility Officials noted that the
unarmed *Xenon Lightning 54* is currently the
most valuable vessel ever seized by outlaws,
worth an astonishing 3.5 trillion Standard Units.

Imperial Warlord Dimitri Verhovnyi denounced
the brazen crime from the Outer Reaches Palace
on Titan this morning.

Io Research Station Astronomers have been
unable to detect the telltale ion trails from the
missing craft, leading some to speculate that the
pirates may have covered their escape by towing
the stolen vessel rather than operating its
monstrous ion drive engines.

As of this morning, no ransom demands have been received by Refinement Facility Officials. Warlord Syndicate Underwriters have warned that they will pay no more than the customary ransom of 1.75 million Standard Units to recover the vessel.

There are currently no clues as to the location of the mammoth tanker or the identities of the hijackers.

12. Free City University

Keira stopped and stared down yet another long nondescript corridor. "Why are we wandering around Free City University today?" she asked Ryo with some annoyance.

"Well," the old Investigator rubbed his chin for several seconds before pointing down the hallway to the left, "Lev seems to think that even though the lunar traffic control information was destroyed, we may still be able to discover something about what happened on the day of the blast."

"Why would the University have that information?"

Ryo shook his head, "I have no idea, but the case has been stalled since we got back from Dublin over a week ago, so any leads would help."

Keira tugged on his arm, "Are you sure we're on the right floor? I swear that we've gone past this same spot at least once before."

"He said door 1272 in the basement of the School of Advanced Physics, so it could be anywhere around here. Let's go down a floor and see what we can find."

The Ripple In Space-Time

Seventeen minutes later, after following the instructions provided by an unenthusiastic janitor on Sub Level 5, Keira pointed to the long-sought portal in weary victory.

Ryo tapped perfunctorily on the door before pushing it open.

It was a dark office of some sort. Weirdly shimmering light spilled from a large video display that took up most of a worktable on the left side of the room.

The dark silhouette huddled in front of the screen turned to scrutinize the new arrivals.

"Great, you found it; come on in," Lev stood and beckoned them to the table.

"You have an office?" Keira asked as she shuffled carefully into the dark room.

Lev pulled up two more chairs, "It's nothing special, just one of the many doctoral workstations."

Keira slumped onto a chair.

Ryo studied the screen. "What have you got for us?"

Lev sat next to the woman, "After you told me

that the guy that we captured in Dublin erased all of the lunar orbit traffic records around the time of the explosion, I spent a few days trying to figure out another way of discovering what went on at the site."

He pointed to the slowly shifting images on the screen, "It turns out that the University Astronomy Department has five different satellites orbiting the moon right now for various student projects."

"How does that help us?" Keira asked.

"I found out that one of the satellites is just an old cosmic ray detector, so that's worthless to us; but at least two of the others are used by Professor Hendley's Moon Surveying class. We might be lucky enough to find some images of the Sea of Crisis around the time of the blast."

"OH!" Ryo patted Lev's shoulder, "Nice job!"

"I suspect it's going to take awhile," Lev warned, "all of the video is raw footage without searchable timeframes."

Ryo nodded, "You two work on this and I'll be back by lunch time."

Just before he pushed open the door to leave, Ryo glanced back at the two seating together in front of the monitor, "I've got a hunch that I want to check out."

• • •

Ryo traveled across the drizzly Quad to the soaring edifice that housed the School of Biology. He had been to this building several times before and wouldn't have any problem finding the proper room.

Compared to the arcane and forbidding School of Advanced Physics basement, the towering Life Sciences Complex was cheery and well lit. Ryo slipped into the bustling Department of Advanced Applied Molecular Biology Office on the twelfth floor. A half dozen energetic students were fluttering merrily about between some sort of group project involving green algae and a jovial middle-aged man in the center of the room.

The din was quite extraordinary in the overfilled office. Ryo navigated past the young scholars to the big man.

The gentleman's face broadened into a wide grin, "Ryo Trop, damn good to see you!"

"Professor," Ryo bowed slightly, "I'm looking for Zmuda. Can you help me out?"

Just as the Investigator had expected, the good-natured teacher's demeanor turned solemn.

The professor glanced at his busy charges, "Come with me." Before they departed he raised his hands high like a country preacher and shouted to the throng, "Keep working! You're doing great!"

The academic unlocked a nondescript door in the back of the room and led Ryo into a small inner office staffed by a muscular red-bearded man and a petite raven-skinned woman. The two looked up in unison from their paperwork.

"Carry on," the professor nodded to the workers, "we're just passing through." He opened a closet door and slid several coats aside before prying open a well-disguised rear door.

The man stepped through the portal and beckoned Ryo to follow him.

"Welcome to the CRAMP Operations Central Headquarters. To the outside world I'm Professor Malcolm Evans, in here I'm called Lieutenant Zmuda."

"Lieutenant?" Ryo laughed, "The last time I saw you it was Sergeant."

Zmuda shrugged, "I gave myself a promotion."

Ryo studied the spacious and well-organized situation room, "It's been awhile since I've needed your encyclopedic knowledge of the clandestine and I seem to have forgotten what CRAMP stands for, although it does come up periodically at the Inquisitor's Office."

"Combat Ready Advanced Mission Personnel. As you may recall, we're a group of concerned citizens of Free City, mostly academics and scientists with a few paramilitarists thrown in, determined to return all of humanity to the high ideals of the past."

"Who are those two in the other room?" Ryo wondered.

"Jasper and Mixion? They're part of the CRAMP. I used an unusual new procedure to clone them as adults in the Advanced Biology lab about a year ago from some genetic information that I found in a really old database."

Ryo was perplexed, "There are plenty of human clones in Free City, myself included, why fiddle around with old stock?"

Zmuda smiled, "Their DNA isn't registered anywhere. If they happen to lose a toenail clipping or maybe an eyelash or two while carrying out a covert operation, no Investigator would ever be able to track them down."

Ryo chuckled, "So you're making my job harder?"

"Not really, none of our especially nasty projects are in Free City. Right now the good stuff involves insurrection and resource reallocation in the fiefdoms.

The old Investigator laughed, "Technically the Inquisitor's Office regards the CRAMP Operation as subversive, not insurrectionist." Ryo loved the lively back and forth with his cloak-and-dagger friend, "The difference centers around the presumption that you hold antiestablishment views but you haven't killed anyone yet."

"Oh but we have Mr. Trop. CRAMP Operatives did in Madame Kufuzu at the Trade Conference in New Rome less than a month ago."

"Why would you guys bother knocking off one of the many wives of the Warlord of EurAfrica?"

Lieutenant Zmuda smiled fiendishly, "Daniel Kufuzu is absurdly well-protected and we need some of his DNA for a cleaver little assassination effort that the CRAMP is putting together. So we bumped off his wife and collected some residual samples from her corpse. I've got the specimens in the lab right now."

"Do I really want to know the details?" Ryo asked half jokingly.

Zmuda's eyebrows arched up, "I'll tell you anyhow as part of this proposed bargain: I'll supply you with whatever information that you came looking for today and you will let me know if anyone in the Inquisitor's Office pins Madame Kufuzu's untimely death on the CRAMP."

Ryo thought for several seconds about the ramifications of the deal, "OK, I'm in."

"Excellent;" a smug smile crossed his face, "my colleagues and I are developing something that we call the x-pathogen, which shows promise in infecting only a single individual with deadly results. It's still very crude, but we hope to use it or something like it to eventually end the current feudal system and allow all humans to live freely again."

"Lofty goals," Ryo nodded. "Tell me about pirates, particularly anything that you might know about two characters named Olin Gristle and Bosco Kremerling."

"Why is it that pirates always end up with the best names?" Zmuda scratched his head for several seconds, "I'm not familiar with either of those two, but it's been a few years since I've done any field work in the Asteroid Belt where they all seem to congregate."

78

Ryo slouched in defeat.

"Why the interest in these two low lives?"

"They paid off a Lunar Traffic Controller to destroy some records on the day that the Ultra Energy Lab was obliterated."

"Dr. Fesai was a dear friend of mine," Zmuda winced. "I have a strange feeling that Daniel Kufuzu or perhaps his step brother Dimitri Verhovnyi are involved with these pirates due to their past misdeeds with some of the roving marauders."

"Alright, I'll look into that," the Investigator smiled.

After several minutes of light banter, Ryo followed the big man back into the student-filled main office. He watched with quiet amusement as Lieutenant Zmuda returned to his alternate persona as Professor Malcolm Evans.

"Ah, you've done a fabulous job!"

As Ryo slogged back between the two Science buildings, he mentally manipulated the scraps of information that the Lieutenant had supplied to him. Why would either of the Warlords that Zmuda mentioned be connected to the destruction of the Ultra Energy Lab that was funded by the Warlord Syndicate of which they were both members?

Still deep in thought, Ryo pushed open the door to the dim Physics Department workroom where he had left his cohorts. In the stark light of the desktop display, he spotted Keira hastily pull her hand away from Lev's.

The two dallying detectives turned in unison towards him, a monochrome lunar image stood frozen on the desktop screen.

"What did you two find?"

Keira sheepishly shifted her chair away from Lev's and gestured for Ryo to join them.

The old Investigator examined the still photo of a colossal smooth charcoal-gray crater depressed in the center of mottled slate and silver-colored highlands. Dozens of smaller dimples pockmarked the surrounding surface.

Lev's finger traced the huge lunar basin; "This is the Sea of Crisis about 27 minutes before the explosion." He pointed to an incongruous beige rectangle on one side of the depression, "Here's the Ultra Energy Lab, or at least the part that's above the surface."

Ryo frowned at the image, "That's not much help."

"From this high up, you can't pick out any details," Keira noted, "but the picture quality is good enough that we can zoom in to a resolution of about ten square centimeters."

Lev brushed the toolbar and the beige rectangle grew to fill most of the screen. A strangely out of place black speck was perched on one corner of the massive structure.

"What's that thing?" Ryo wondered.

Lev manipulated the controls until the dark anomaly occupied the entire display.

"We were looking at this earlier," Keira tilted her head to the side, "it's some sort of unusual spacecraft."

Ryo nodded slowly, "I think that's an Ore Runner, although it doesn't look anything like the Lunar variant." He pondered it for nearly a minute. "I've got an idea that might pan out for us. Lev, send this image off for me."

The young man slid his fingers over the toolbar, "Where to?"

The older man leaned forward and entered the address of the Vessel Registry Bureau, "Inspector Ryo Trop, ID 783682. Identify craft and detail current status and location."

Several seconds later the stark lunar image was replaced by a crisp registration photo of the spacecraft in dry-dock. A long scrolling description filled the bottom of the screen: *Vessel identified as the Butin Belle. Special Midget Ore Runner Class 37a. Construction completed on 13th of November 2429 at the Vesta Ship Works. Currently registered to Celestial Delivery Systems, Mariner Station, Mars. Hijacked by unknown individuals on 12th of February, 2445. Present location unknown.*

"Pirates again," Ryo muttered.

Keira looked up at him, "What does *Butin Belle* mean?"

Ryo shook his head, "I don't know; it's French, I think."

"Beautiful loot," Lev chuckled.

13. Titan Palace

Saturn was slowly rising above the horizon.

Dimitri Verhovnyi stared through one of the many thick plate glass windows of the palace at the shimmering sliver of the monstrous gas giant as it grew ever-larger. Soon the stupendous rings would edge into view and the majestic planet would gradually shift from a glowering red to a more pleasing pinkish-orange as it climbed higher to dominate the hazy sky of Titan.

At around nine and a half times further from the Sun than the Earth, Saturn was a far brighter and more imposing presence on the huge moon than the distant and unremarkable yellow star over 1.4 billion kilometers away at the center of the Solar System.

Somewhere out there in the vastness where the imbeciles that he had engaged to carry out his schemes.

Pirates, Dimitri scornfully noted, were not known for following instructions and his two bands of marauders were no exception.

After weeks of trying, the Kuiper Belt Shipjacks had finally managed to commandeer an unarmed and unmanned space tanker that he intended to use as a base for his secret operations. To avoid detection, it was now creeping slowly towards the Asteroid Belt. Gristle's Raiders had acquired the materials and skilled laborers that he would need from the Moon but not without using far too much force and explosives for what should have been a stealthy undertaking.

Now the Free City Inquisitor's Office was snooping about for the cause of the blast.

"Idiots!"

The great ringed planet took up most of the eastern sky now. A jagged bluish electrical storm swirled sinisterly around the southern pole.

A knock at the door interrupted his fretting. His eleven-year-old parlormaid peered leerily into the suite.

The girl was one of his many household scrubs; in a year or two, he'd profit nicely by selling her off to the Sex Slavers.

"Excuse me Master," she bowed nervously, "I have your breakfast, if it pleases you now."

"Yes," he growled tersely, "bring it in."

The little wretch set the tray of food on his dining table and hurried off.

Dimitri watched the girl leave. She was obviously afraid of him, he had a well-deserved reputation that he had cultivated over many years for brawling fits of rage. But he had always treated his servants and slaves with cool detachment, especially the half dozen or so girls that made up the domestic staff.

He sat and consumed the meal.

His long dead mother, after all, had been forced into sex slavery. She'd been one of the many wives of Jonathan Kufuzu until she displeased the third Warlord of EurAfrica and was sold off as carnal fodder to Dimitri's despicable father, Lord Pavel Verhovnyi. At forty-two years old, she unintentionally produced Pavel's only child before killing herself on the lethal surface of Titan.

Unwelcome from birth, Dimitri was sent away as a baby to be raised by the subjugated drudges in the barely habitable selenium mines kilometers below the frozen surface of the massive moon of Saturn. As he grew up amongst the despondent and miscreant miners in the cold and dark labyrinths, Dimitri vowed vengeance against his father who had pompously declared himself the first Imperial Warlord of the Outer Reaches.

After years of plotting and planning, he'd snuck into the newly constructed Titan Palace as a teenager and stabbed his father to death.

Two days later, after murdering most of the old man's advisors, Dimitri enthroned himself as the Supreme Warlord and took over the now vast fiefdom.

His father's frozen and mutilated corpse still dangled from a tall picket in front of the palace as a grisly reminder of Dimitri's ruthlessness.

But he had other scores to settle.

Even though he was a reluctant member of the Warlord Syndicate and continued to pay the onerous dues to the trade organization, he felt no sympathy towards the six other squabbling autocrats that made up the group. The Asteroid Belt and Jupiter Colonies Fiefdom was merely a weak and unorganized collection of a few widely spread outposts led by an oblivious figurehead Warlord on Vesta. The Fiefdoms of Mars and the Moon were both pleasant paradises compared to the difficult and isolated hell of the Outer Reaches.

Dimitri had nothing in common with the three pampered sovereigns of Earth; with large and compliant populations, copious resources and an agreeable atmosphere, they had no understanding of the adversities that Off-Worlders constantly faced.

He had an especially strong hatred for his

stepbrother, Daniel Kufuzu. The EurAfrican Warlord had taken over for his vile father years ago and had refused to acknowledge Dimitri as a blood relative.

Dimitri sneered with contempt; soon he would inflect a horrible revenge on the Kufuzu family.

His own fiefdom had grown wealthier and more formidable in recent years and would soon surpass the status of Mars and rival that of IndoPacifica on the Earth.

Nearly twenty different mines and the huge new Kuiper Gas Refinement Facility produced vast riches for him. He had an army of "tax" and bribe collectors in his employ but his tireless slavers generated far more profits than his other endeavors. Dimitri's methodical thugs would "arrest" hapless squatters in the far-flung outposts and drag them off to the Warlord's forced labor facilities to work off trumped up debits that could seemingly never be satisfied.

Dimitri pushed his nearly empty plate aside; the last scraps would undoubtedly be consumed by his skinny little parlormaid. He chuckled to himself, she would be worth more with some meat on her bones.

He swaggered back to the window and listened to the latest message from the *Butin Belle*, "This *is bluebird calling big boy. We are in sight of the winter house but the lightning has not arrived. Your package is ready to Air Mail but we need the address."*

Excellent, he thought, perhaps Gristle and his brain-dead First Mate could actually get things right.

Dimitri began his reply, "Use the smallest midget to deliver the package to my brother for arrival in one month. Half a klick makes the biggest noise. Have the guests work on the new products when the lightning appears."

Saturn had nearly reached its zenith in the Titan sky.

He smiled fleetingly at the immense ringed planet before sending off the dispatch; soon his palace would be filled with fawning half-wits.

14. News Item:
Lunar Lab investigation continues

*Dateline: 20th of June, 2445; Free City
Inquisitor's Office, Free City, Earth*

Chief Inspector Helga Bennet of the Inquisitor's
Office offered an update this morning on the
ongoing investigation into last month's
unexplained destruction of the Lunar Ultra
Energy Research Laboratory.

Citing unnamed sources in the Mining Guild,
Bennet dispelled the widely held notion that the
disaster which claimed 287 lives was caused by
illegal mining operations below the Sea of
Crises. She also put to rest a rival theory
regarding careless handling of the unstable
antimatter that had been produced in great
quantities at the facility in recent years. Inspector
Bennet spent many minutes detailing the
elaborate safety measures used by the staff of the
doomed research station.

"The Inquisitor's Office is now quite certain that
the destruction of the Lab was not an accident,"
the Chief Inspector said.

"We have discovered some detailed lunar
surveillance images from the day of the incident

and our best people are studying them very carefully for clues," Bennet assured reporters.

When asked about possible suspects, the Chief indicated that the Inquisitor's Office is currently seeking two persons of interest for questioning.

Bennet concluded the interview by emphasizing her confidence in the detective work being carried out by the Office.

15. Keira Norton after hours

She was finally back in her minuscule Free City apartment.

Keira wearily stripped off her soiled eveningwear and slumped in despair onto her unmade sofa bed. She was alone in her dim apartment, which certainly wasn't how she had imagined the date with Lev would end.

She sighed in frustration. The tantalizing spark of attraction that they had shared together in the dark School of Physics workroom had been largely extinguished in her mind by the disastrous outing.

Keira crawled under the rumpled covers and began to methodically review the star-crossed date.

She'd met Lev hours earlier at a period-themed nightspot called the *Waimea Surf Society and Bar*. The establishment was well known for its collection of ancient and obscure dance music. To her dismay, most of the other women at the club were attired in glitzy and revealing swimwear while she had come sensibly clad in a subdued woolen frock entirely appropriate for the drizzly evening weather.

The Ripple In Space-Time

Even though Lev was outfitted in colorful beach shorts and a flashy Polynesian shirt, he assured her that she would fit in with the high-spirited crowd.

More than a few other revelers had scoffed disapprovingly in her direction during the evening.

An hour into the rendezvous, after consuming far too much alcohol in a back booth with Lev, she'd been cajoled into venturing out onto the dance floor.

It was the lone pleasurable interlude of the evening, Keira realized.

She'd clung drunkenly to him during a seductive and swirlingly slow instrumental. Her hands crept up his muscled back and glided through his soft black curls. Even now, hours later, Keira could recall his inviting scent.

But eventually the song and the intimate erotic fantasy ended.

Keira had held him close for far too long when the sedate instrumental was replaced by a snappy song. Lev twirled apart from her with an embarrassed grin. While the others around her bounced and spun to the catchy tune, Keira stood alone in jilted disbelief.

The ditzy lyrics were still stuck in her head,
"and she'll have fun, fun, fun till her daddy takes
the T'bird away."

Lev coaxed her into dancing again but it wasn't
the same. As she tried to keep up with the
energetic crowd, the lyrics seemed to mock her
many missteps and blunders, *"You look like ace*
now, you look like an ace...."

The jostling and gyrating had caused the excess
of alcohol in her stomach to make itself painfully
known. When it had threatened to spew out,
Keira sprinted away to the lavatory in panic.

As she huddled over the commode vomiting, she
could hear the revelers on the dance floor
stomping and cheering at end of the ancient surf
song.

She cleaned herself up and crept back to their
booth.

To her horror, she watched from the distant
vantage point as Lev merrily danced with a
plump blonde woman who popped repeatedly
out of her too-tight bikini bra.

Why had he abandoned her for some trollop at
the first signs of trouble?

When the tune ended, Lev beckoned to her to
join them but Keira shook her head in dread.

She certainly didn't want to risk being cast by the catty regulars as the dowdy chick that retched all over the dance floor.

Perhaps she had imagined the little glint of understanding in Lev's eyes as he stood there. After several seconds of staring at her from across the dance floor, he trotted back to her.

"This is Desiree!" He had tugged the sparsely clad woman to the booth with him, "Des was my first housemate and I haven't seen her in months!"

Lev slid into the booth and gestured for Desiree to join them. The heavyset beach babe complied.

"Des this is Keira. Keira this is Desiree."

The chubby interloper smiled, "Hi Keira! I hear that you two are working together on that awful mess at the Moon base." Desiree stroked Lev's shoulder fondly, "Are you a grad student too?"

"No, I have a real job with the Free City Fiefdom Liaison Office," she'd replied curtly.

"Oh," Desiree shook her head disdainfully, "that doesn't sound like much fun."

"Des is an amazing artist. She painted fantastic murals all over the walls at my house."

As she laughed at his flattery, her jiggling breasts threatened to break free of the insufficient fabric that restrained them. "Hey, you two; I've got some really excellent *katchah*. Do you want some?"

"Sure," Lev chirped, "I'll take a bit."

Keira had frowned disapprovingly, "None for me."

Katchah was one of dozens of illegal and mildly hallucinogenic herbs that filtered into the counter culture of Free City from the lawless domains of the Warlords. Years ago, Keira's own antiestablishment parents had been nabbed when they imported several kilos of the banned substance. They had paid a substantial fine for the transgression and nearly lost their coveted Importer's License.

Keira winced; even now her parents continued to sneak the profitable contraband across the border despite her repeated admonishments.

Desiree produced a thin and elaborately decorated pouch from her bikini bottom. Her stubby fingers retrieved a sticky hunk of shredded brown leaves and she held it temptingly in front of Lev.

He eagerly snapped up the offering and kissed Desiree's cheek in thanks. She pressed a small lump into her own mouth.

The drug seemed to cause her table partners to fixate on each other. As the evening wore on, they spoke less and less to her and more and more to each other in progressively more incomprehensible and slurred sentences.

Finally when her queasiness had subsided, Keira left them chortling gleefully at their own terrible jokes.

She'd whimpered gloomily in the nearly empty transport back to her apartment building.

Why had she been attracted to Lev in the first place?

He was self-indulgent and often maddeningly unfocused, not unlike her parents, Keira realized with a start. He seemed far more interested in immediate gratification than long-term fulfillment. Perhaps that was why he had apparently selected Desiree's offer of quick thrills to her own possibilities of eventual stability and perhaps even love.

In the dark and quiet apartment bed, Keira pressed her eyes tightly closed; he was completely wrong for her and she should just get on with other more promising matters.

But still, she sighed heavily, there was just something special about Lev.

16. A lamentable lack of mirth

Jana floated aimlessly in her dark and miserable cell.

She drew her attention back to the matter at hand, "Or, if there were a sympathy in choice, War, death, or sickness did lay siege to it, Making it momentany as a sound."

This was the sixth recital of *A Midsummer Night's Dream* that she'd forced herself to endure since she'd been taken hostage. Three and a half decades earlier it had been her favorite work of Shakespeare, now she would have done almost anything to enjoy *Much Ado About Nothing* or *Macbeth* instead.

Where was she?

Jana chortled at the irony of the question; she was lost in the Solar System and lost in *A Midsummer Night's Dream*.

A midsummer night in the Solar System....

Jana stiffened in dread; she was losing her mind.

OK, keep going.

The Ripple In Space-Time

She took a deep breath, "Swift as a shadow,

short as any dream, Brief as the lightning in the collied night."

Jana cackled hoarsely; she remembered a naive girl in the back row of her Ancient English Lit class asking the Professor if a 'collied night' had something to do with sheepdogs shepherding in the evening.

Regrettably her tenuous focus was waning; she would have to come back to Shakespeare later.

She tapped her fingertips to her thumb and tallied up weeks. It was late June or perhaps early July. Far off on the hospitable blue Earth, someone was surely enjoying a genuine midsummer's night.

Hopefully Lev had adjusted to her disappearance. She dearly missed the long distance daily chit-chat that they had shared; she describing the intricacies and intrigue of her classified research and he chronicling his gregarious social interactions and his newfound pursuit of fun.

Jana's shoulders slumped in despair; she had lost everything and everyone with no prospect of regaining either.

He had been gifted from the beginning, she reminisced. As a two-year-old, Lev would toddle

98

around their townhouse in Free City and methodically describe everything that he saw in startling detail, 'Mommy, this is the parlor. The walls are white. Under the gray sofa is a yellow ball with light blue stripes and big red stars. Out of the window, I can see the transports on Breton Street.'

A keen sense of the physical world had come easily to him, social skills had not.

In those aspects, they had been the same; Jana winced. She had quite willingly forgone the long and uncertain path of romance for the solitude of a predictable and secure life as a Physicist.

When the task of completing her education had been achieved, she methodically set about producing a child.

Jana had eschewed all of the ordinary complex social interactions with men and instead chose to be clinically inseminated with the genetic material of an anonymous and randomly selected academic from the University.

Brainy parents had begat a brilliant son, she wryly noted.

When he was young she had dutifully carted him off to peewee football and preteen art classes. They had both struggled mightily to interact with their peers at the sports venues and art studios; neither had much luck.

Just as she had done in Buenos Aires many years earlier, Lev excelled in school. While he spent progressively more time studying the complexities of Literature, Mathematics and especially the Sciences, she had been drawn further into her own pursuit of Ultra Energy Physics. He had earned a High School diploma with highest honors just as she had been awarded a Nobel Prize in Physics.

Lev had of course attended Free City University.

In his second year he'd sat through the final class that she'd taught as a Senior Professor before accepting a staff researcher's position at the small High Energy Lab in the Physics Department basement. Not surprisingly he had easily earned the highest marks in the huge lecture hall of over three hundred students.

When he started his graduate studies, Jana was promoted to the Chief Researcher's position at the Lunar Ultra Energy Lab.

After she'd left Earth, he'd wandered off course.

People told her that she should be dismayed by his supposed failings, but she knew better. After more than twenty years of excelling at academics he was finally delving into the much more difficult to fathom subtleties of human interactions.

Lev's long string of girlfriends and casual lovers had much more to do with systematically comparing different female personas than promiscuity.

Eventually he would settle on one that he liked, she chuckled.

Jana wriggled around and floated to the porthole. The view was exactly the same as it had been for days: hundreds of gray asteroids slowly tumbled together through cold dark space.

Wait!

She pressed her cheek against the frigid window and strained to resolve the tiny anomaly.

There was color!

A minuscule red speck flashed on and off at the extreme limit of what Jana could see through the porthole. It was a ship of some kind, she finally decided.

For hours Jana studied the approaching vessel until the strain in her neck and the immense craft's slow trajectory past the *Butin Belle* made further viewing impossible.

"I saw something!" she blurted out to Bosco as he dragged her backwards through the dim passageway.

"Yes you did, you old hag." He tugged her past a thick bulkhead door.

Her hands were tightly bound behind her back but Jana managed to twist around to see him. At this point, even the crude and volatile thug was preferable to the slow numbing madness of prolonged solitude. "Can I call you Bosco?"

"Boz," a twitchy half smile darted across his scruffy face.

"It was a ship, wasn't it Boz."

He stopped at a closed hatchway and spun her around to face him, "It's the *Lightning*."

Jana watched him slide his fingertips over the door's security interface. If she ever escaped from her cell, this was as far as she'd get without being detected.

"It was supposed to be here weeks ago," Bosco yanked open the door, "but the lugheads that hijacked it couldn't figure out how to board a robotic ship." He rolled his eyes contemptuously, "Shipjacks, my ass!"

Jana's senses were slowly returning, "Why are we and the *Lightning* out here in the middle of nowhere, Boz?"

He stared unnervingly at her for several seconds, "You talk too much."

Jana forced a smile; if she was ever going to manipulate the pirates they would have to view her as benign and friendly. "Sorry, I'm just really happy to chat with someone."

"We're gonna get you back together with your friends later today," Boz pulled her gruffly into the control room, "you can talk all you want with them."

"Ah, Doctor Fesai," Captain Gristle said, "it's good to see you again."

Bosco secured her binding straps to the side of a stout control panel before propelling himself out of the pilothouse.

As Jana watched the Captain tend to the controls, she resolved to trick him into revealing more information to her. "When are we docking with the *Lightning*?"

He looked up at her with some annoyance.

She smiled innocently at the man.

"In about an hour if everything goes right," the Captain studied a small display, "then we'll move you and the others on to the *Xenon Lightning* and put you to work."

Jana suppressed the tightening sense of dread that threatened to overwhelm her. "What do you want us to do, Mr. Gristle?" she asked cheerily.

"Our employer would like you fabricate some devices using those matter/antimatter pairings that we brought along from the Moon lab."

"OH," she nodded, "I'm sure we could do that for you guys."

Jana's heart was racing; the pirates would almost certainly want her to produce some sort of small and very destructive weapons with the dangerous and finicky materials. If she could win their confidence to the point that they became lax about overseeing her, she might be able to thwart their efforts.

Far down the passageway, Jana could hear Boz jostling about with one of the bulkhead doors.

• • •

Bosco shoved the two young deckhands out of the way as he blustered into the large compartment, "I told you morons to stay away from this friggin' thing!" He studied the robust basketball-sized sphere clamped into the launching fixture of the deployment bay.

"It's worth more than both of you lowlifes put together."

His hands slid over the warm smooth surface of the object, it had an odd magnetic-like quality that clamped his palms firmly to it. Boz couldn't fathom why the contents of the orb behaved in this way, but he savored the strange sensation nevertheless.

The deckhands watched with some amusement as the burly second in command struggled to jerk his hands away from the device.

Boz floated to the storage rack and studied the profusion of messenger tugs that were kept there. An unforeseen benefit of hijacking a ship that was outfitted as a delivery vessel was the large supply of the tiny expendable vehicles onboard that were used to nudge packages from the passing ship to customers waiting below on the surface of a planet or moon.

He selected the smallest long-distance/dense atmosphere tug on the rack. Boz pried open the hatch of the grapefruit-sized robot and entered the destination coordinates. He sealed the device and pressed it against the larger object sitting in the launch fixture. The two machines clung together.

Bosco smiled briefly at the interlocked spheres before gesturing towards the door.

The crewman followed him obediently out of the deployment bay.

• • •

Jana pressed the 'send' button in panic.

She stared at the open hatchway as Olin Gristle propelled himself back in to the control room. He had been gone for perhaps a minute, but she had managed to squirm awkwardly around and hastily tap out a message on the communication console. Hopefully it was on its way to the intended recipient right now.

Jana smiled innocently to the Captain as he returned, but fortunately he was preoccupied with the handheld display that he carried.

After several seconds of holding her breath in fear, she finally relaxed; apparently she'd gotten away with the little misdeed.

A worn-out old crewman peered into the control room.

"Excuse me, Sir," the scarred and grizzled pirate beckoned, "we have the men prisoners."

Captain Gristle waved them into the cramped room.

The elderly crewman led the downcast chain gang consisting of four of her colleagues from the Lab into the pilothouse. The first was an unlucky janitor who happened to be in the Containment Facility when the kidnappers had forced their entry.

Jana studied the others with dismay.

Her gifted assistant Erik seemed to have suffered some sort of breakdown; his terror-stricken eyes leapt around with swirling incomprehension. A chubby teenage intern stared pleadingly at her; the poor fellow had arrived at the Lab about a week before the catastrophe. The last of the miserable lot was Ramesh, a haphazardly grad student who had helped out with her research. He grinned briefly in recognition as he was pulled roughly past her.

The old pirate prodded the shackled newcomers into a tight group around Jana.

Boz appeared at the hatchway and nodded to Gristle, "It's ready."

The Captain rubbed his chin hesitantly before operating several switches on the control panel.

The Ripple In Space-Time

An alarm sounded for several seconds before a faint whirring pervaded the *Butin Belle*.

When a green indicator flashed, Captain Gristle looked up at the hapless hostages, "With that task complete, we can get on with other misdoings." He surveyed the tattered group. "I hope that the cruise has been a pleasant one."

"Well...." Ramesh started.

Jana shook her head in alarm and he stifled any further comment.

Gristle glared at the man before continuing, "You are now slaves and you will be treated as such. Misbehavior on your part will result in torture or death." He balled his fist and struck Ramesh hard in the stomach.

The young man doubled over in agony.

The others watched in horrified silence.

"Shortly," Gristle continued, "you will be transferred onto the *Xenon Lightning* where you will beginning producing several items required by our employer."

Bosco chuckled cynically at the hatchway.

The Captain stared ominously at Jana, "I expect nothing less than your full cooperation."

S F Chapman

17. News Item:
New speed standard announced

Dateline: 6th of July, 2445; Free City, Earth

With spacecraft speeds climbing ever higher and a confusing hodgepodge of systems to measure that velocity still persisting from the early days of space travel, The Free City Standards Committee has announced a new and definitive benchmark for indicating spacecraft speeds.

Upon the hoped for universal adoption of the standard, gone forever will be such arcane and archaic nomenclature such as kilometers per second, knots, parsecs per year or even the ancient miles per hour still used in the backwaters of the Outer Reaches.

After years of exhaustive study and no small amount of machinations, the Committee announced that the standard of spacecraft speed measurement will be Astronomical Units per year or more simply AU/yr.

Some variation of Astronomical Units have been used by Astronomers since the time of the ancient Greeks. Nearly all young students of the sciences in Free City know that an Astronomical Unit is the approximate mean distance from the Sun to the Earth, or a little less than 150 million kilometers.

The new system easily accommodates the leisurely lunar escape velocity of 0.8 AU/yr, the customary traveling speed of most space freighters at about 16 AU/yr and the blistering velocities of the newest fast interceptors of over 45 AU/yr.

If approved by the Warlord Syndicate and the Free City Spacecraft Authority, the new standard will take full effect by the 9th of April 2450.

18. The ripple

"There's one," Dr. Carla Stuhr pointed to the dappled and brightly colored image on the monitor.

Lev nodded, "OK, I see it."

In the dimly lit basement workroom, both Ryo and Keira strained to detect the indistinguishable irregularity.

Finally the old Investigator shrugged, "You got me, what are we looking for here?"

"Now I lost it," Carla admitted sheepishly. The fledgling Gravitational Astronomer adjusted the sensitivity and the image exploded into a chaotic mosaic of vivid specks. She gently manipulated the controls until the countless colored dots merged into larger irregular splotches.

"There, that's better." The tall brown haired scientist turned to the visitors in triumph, "I bumped into Lev several days ago and he mentioned that he was helping out with your investigation of the Lab disaster."

"I told Dr. Stuhr that we weren't having much luck tracking down the pirates who were apparently at the Lab just before the explosion," Lev interjected.

Carla laughed girlishly, "It seems so strange when you call me Dr. Stuhr, sweetie."

Lev blushed.

"How is it that you two know each other?" Ryo asked.

Keira rubbed her forehead in distaste at the nauseatingly flirtatious pair.

Carla grinned, "We dated for awhile, then I moved in with him for about six months. It wasn't particularly serious."

"Why am I not surprised," Keira muttered to herself.

Lev kissed Carla's cheek; "She finally traded me in for someone else."

Ryo spent several seconds studying each of the three young people in room, "Alright then; back to the matter at hand. Please explain the significance of the abstract art on the screen, Dr. Stuhr."

"What we're looking at is an enhanced false color image of gravitational waves propagating through the Solar System."

112

Keira grimaced, "Gravitational waves?"

"The physics involved is really complicated," Lev admitted. "Mmm, you need to know something about Space-Time for this to make any sense."

"That's true," Carla nodded, "I'd forgotten that most people have never heard of it."

Ryo and Keira shared the same befuddled look.

Lev smiled, "It's not that bad, Albert Einstein was remarkably good at using simple analogies to explain parts of the theories of relativity. So imagine a bed sheet pulled tightly over a frame."

Ryo tipped his head slightly and Keira frowned.

"This could be an overly simplified two-dimensional version of four-dimensional Space-Time. If we place an object like a bowling ball on the fabric, the mass of the object bends the sheet just as a star or a planet 'bends' Space-Time."

"I suppose that makes sense," the old Investigator stroked his chin.

"A small object like a asteroid barely bends the fabric," Lev continued, "a really massive star creates a significant distortion that extends far beyond. Gravity is the bending or warping of Space-Time."

"What does this have to do with gravitational waves?" Keira scowled.

"So far, in the sheet analogy," Carla chuckled, "our bowling ball is at rest. Out there in the Universe, everything is moving."

"This is my favorite part," Lev grinned. "If I nudge the bowling ball and it rolls around on our tightly stretched sheet, it bends the fabric around it as it moves causing distinctive waves or ripples that effect anything that is nearby. If it passes near a smaller ball, the little guy will fall into orbit around the bigger one. The same thing happens in space with stars, planets and moons; even galaxies. Moving objects with mass cause ripples in Space-Time that we can detect as gravitational waves."

Ryo slowly smiled, "OK, I see how that works."

"For centuries," Carla tapped idly at colorful image on the display screen, "we knew that gravitational waves existed, but they are so faint that we couldn't detect them."

"Just in the last thirty years," Lev interjected, "the University finally developed a really good Gravitational Observatory satellite which peers down from way above the center of the Solar System. The equipment in the Astronomy Lab filters out the nearly overpowering gravitational waves from the sun, the planets and all of the larger moons, leaving just the small and really strange stuff that zips about through space."

Carla smiled in triumph, "That's what I work with as the junior researcher for the Solar System Gravitational Anomalies Project."

Ryo shook his head in confusion, "I still have no idea of how this connects to our investigation."

"I'm sorry," Carla apologized, "Lev has a way of knocking me off track. As we just talked about with the sheet analogy, when mass moves through Space-Time it causes a distortion or bending that we see here as a ripple; the higher the mass and speed, the bigger the ripple or wave. Currently our research group is looking at the high speed and high mass exosolar particles that constantly stream through the Solar System."

Lev interrupted the Astronomer, "Tiny fast moving bits of really heavy junk that get spit out of big stars when they explode."

Keira squinted at the brightly colored screen, "Is there much of that stuff whizzing around?"

"There are always some massive particles. If a star supernovas in our section of the galaxy, the constant trickle turns into a torrent for a few weeks." Carla's fingers glided over the speckled screen, "We can't detect high speed electrons or muons, mainly because their mass is so low, but we can spot nearly anything else, especially if it is moving at more than a couple of kilometers per second.

Ryo scrutinized the image, "What's that little trail?"

Dr. Stuhr glanced at the monitor, "Judging by the color and the slight curve of the tracing, I'd guess it's most likely a few alpha particles that are zipping along at about a third of the speed of light. We can request a detailed velocity and mass analysis if you want to know for sure."

"I think we're OK," Ryo smiled at the scientist. "What is it that you found for us, Ms Stuhr?"

"Ah, I recorded a peculiar observation about a month ago," Carla summoned a new image to the screen, "I was right in the middle of a transitional metal ion study at the time, so I saved it for future scrutiny."

A fuzzy and slowly moving group of a few sparkling yellow and orange specks produced a noticeable wrinkling of the surrounding gray and brown mottled background on the display.

"This is not normal," she assured them. "None of the other researchers has ever seen anything like it. The tight grouping of the dots and the relatively slow speed suggests that this is a spacecraft carrying a small quantity of unusually dense material."

"Maybe it's a bulk freighter loaded with Uranium?" Keira wondered.

"It seems to be a much smaller ship with just a tiny amount of stuff onboard that's really heavy."

Lev tapped at the brightly shimmering cloud on the screen, "What's the density of these little guys, Carla?"

She toggled the controls to freeze the image and several numbers appeared next to the splotches. "This one has a density of about 32,000 grams per cubic centimeter and is moving along at 120 kilometers per second."

"Wow!" Lev exclaimed. "I recall that Uranium is only about 19 grams per cubic centimeter."

"What is this then?" Ryo pondered.

"Could it be a cluster of mini black holes?" Lev guessed.

"No, that would be so rare as to be unheard of," Carla concluded, "even the smallest black hole would warp Space-Time much more than these things. The gravitational effects upon everything in the Solar System would also be quite noticeable. This is something else."

"Neutron-degenerate matter maybe," Lev asked hopefully.

"Neutron what?" Keira asked.

"The super compact material that makes up Neutron stars, and no it's considerably less condensed than that." Carla made several calculations and frowned, "The density of this particular speck here works out to be roughly equivalent a grain of sand with a mass of a bowling ball."

"So it's probably some really weird super heavy ordinary matter," Lev nodded.

Ryo squinted at the fuzzy image, "I believe that's what they were cooking up at the Ultra Energy Lab."

"Exactly," Carla smiled, "that's why I thought you'd be interested in this information."

"Where was this load of strange and possibly stolen cargo headed?" the old Investigator asked.

118

"Unfortunately we only captured a few hours of observations weeks ago and we haven't seen anything since, perhaps because they've stopped moving; I'd guess the Asteroid Belt in the vicinity of Lutetia." She tapped her fingertip against her forehead, "But they could be as far away as Jupiter's Trojan Asteroids at this point."

"Thanks, it's not much to go on," Ryo sighed.

The warble of a communication device interrupted the group discussion. Lev stared at his display in disbelief.

"What is it?" Keira asked in concern.

"It must be a joke," Lev frowned, "although I'm not sure who would be this cruel."

Ryo gently twisted the taciturn man's hand around and slowly read the short message aloud, *"LEV...I...ON...BU...BEL, MA."*

Lev squinted his now misty eyes. "It's my mom," he stared at the tiny screen with growing resolve, "she's still alive!"

Ryo pried the device from the man and methodically checked the particulars of the cryptic dispatch, "It was sent about twenty-five minutes ago from an unidentified source somewhere near the boundary of the Outer Reaches."

"Ryo," Keira stared at the old Investigator, "Could 'BU BEL' be the *Butin Belle*?"

He hoisted the communication device up in front of the frozen image of the unusual ripple in Space-Time that they had been studying in earnest. "Yes, I suspect that we've just stumbled upon two clues here."

During the next twenty minutes, Keira uploaded Carla's information to the Inquisitor's Office and Ryo contacted Helga to share the startling new evidence.

Lev stood stiffly considering the ramifications of the revelations amidst the burst of activity.

When she had finished her work, Keira pulled gently at Lev's sleeve and he hesitantly followed her to the door.

"Dr. Stuhr," Ryo turned towards the helpful young Astronomer as the group of investigators shuffled out of the workroom, "please let me know right away if you spot anything like this again."

19. Hot on the trail

Ryo regarded the sparkling trove of billions of stars with interest through the generous front windows of the new craft. He had rarely been in space and with each visit its cold stark beauty had amazed him.

This trip was no exception.

Weeks had dashed by since Dr. Stuhr had alerted them to the peculiar gravitational readings in an obscure section of the Asteroid Belt and Lev had received the unusual message from his mother.

Helga had insisted that Ryo and his team of lucky young cohorts should track down the *Butin Belle* which now seemed likely to contain Jana Fesai, the fugitive pirates and apparently a cache of stolen materials from the Lunar Lab.

To his left, pressed into the Second Mate's seat by the brisk acceleration of the ship, Lev gazed out at the celestial vista. Ryo had noticed that the young man had been clumsily striving to avoid watching Keira as she busied herself at the controls of the impressive and speedy new law enforcement interceptor called the *Seiran*.

Ryo mused that the name of the vessel referred to an elusive and ethereal mist that appeared without warning in the mountains of ancient Japan. With the *Seiran's* speed, stealth and formidable armaments, he hoped to locate and seize the *Butin Belle* undetected.

Now at last they were underway. The powerful engines were quickly pushing the sleek craft away from Earth towards the Lutetia sector of the Asteroid Belt twenty days away.

Keira engaged the autopilot, "There's not much to do now, I'm afraid."

"Ah, but there is," Ryo chortled, "if we are to succeed and hopefully avoid a most painful death at the hands of the pirates, we need to familiarize ourselves with several vital areas of knowledge."

He turned to Lev, "I want you to carefully study all available information about the *Butin Belle*. Hopefully you can discover some weaknesses that could be exploited in its capture."

The young man winced at the burdensome mandate.

Keira smirked wryly at Lev's misfortune.

"You, young lady," Ryo directed in his most paternal voice, "will spend all of your spare time learning the capabilities of the *Seiran*, paying

122

close attention to weaponry and maneuvering abilities. We don't want to be figuring out how to operate the ordnance while the pirates are shooting at us."

She nodded ruefully.

"With Lev's help," Ryo added, "I hope to learn as much as possible about the Tau Atoms that were being produced at the Lunar Lab."

The *Seiran's* speed indictor was rapidly approaching the craft's maximum velocity.

• • •

Dimitri Verhovnyi could restrain himself no longer.

He snickered triumphantly at his superb little secret. With one swift and decisive strike all of humanity would know and fear his name.

The Warlord of the Outer Reaches had been preparing his brutal vengeance against his arrogant half-brother for years and now its fulfill was less than a week away.

He strutted around his chamber in search of some diversion.

Dimitri idly surveyed several routine reports

detailing mining outputs but they seemed so trivial compared to his shrewd plan.

Perhaps an early meal would relax him.

"GIRL!" he bellowed.

His tremulous parlormaid appeared at the door, "Yes Master?"

He leered contemptuously at the pathetic little sprite; he resolved to replace her in the coming months with two or three more pleasing slave girls. "Bring me my supper now!"

She nodded in distress at his command before hurrying off.

• • •

"Alright, I think I understand this now," Ryo frowned as he stared at Lev. "Everything around us is made of 'Electron Atoms' or energy."

"Right," Lev nodded. "The oxygen in the air, the gold in the banks and the calcium in your bones; these are all made of atoms that are composed of only three parts: electrons and the two lightest quarks which are called *up* and *down*. There's some force particles and perhaps some neutrinos, but we'll ignore them."

The old Investigator scratched is head in confusion, "I seem to remember something about protons and neutrons in atoms, how do they fit into this mess?"

The younger man smiled, "Protons and neutrons are made of *up* and *down* quarks. A proton's got two *ups* and one *down*. A neutron has two *downs* and one *up*."

"OK. What about those unusual Tau Atoms that your mom was putting together at the Lunar Ultra Energy Lab?"

"That is what earned her a Nobel Prize," Lev smiled. "Long ago, a few much heavier atoms were put together using two much more massive quarks called *charm* and *strange*."

Ryo laughed, "Who came up with these odd names?"

"I don't remember, but Physicist often have a peculiar sense of humor regarding subatomic particles. Other than the much greater mass, a *charm* quark is essentially identical to an *up* quark and *strange* is identical to *down*. Instead of electrons spinning around the atom, scientists added the identical but much more massive muons; hence the name Mu Atoms. Amazingly, we can bash these parts together and make many types of atoms that are identical to the regular stuff except they're hundreds of times more massive."

"I guess that makes sense."

"Tau atoms were recently built with even heavier quarks called *top* and *bottom,* then surrounded by tauons instead of electrons. There are still only tiny quantities of this stuff and it can be very unstable. It's mainly being studied by researchers for now. Tau atoms are *thousands* of times more massive than their electron atom equivalents."

The old investigator frowned, "Why go to all of the trouble of making super heavy atoms?"

"E=mc2," Lev smirked. "A tiny bit of mass can be converted into a vast amount of energy. The more mass that you can jamb into a small space, the more energy can be released."

"So something that's tiny and very heavy is really just a way of storing a huge amount of energy?"

Lev nodded, "Frightening, yes."

• • •

Fortunately, Jana concluded, Bosco seemed to favor her over the group of her hapless coworkers.

He had dragged her alone through several airlocks and left her more or less unharmed locked away in the gargantuan aft bulk cargo compartment of the *Lightning* with only the feebleminded cabin boy to stand guard.

While the boy had looked on with his dull brown eyes, Jana had quickly surveyed the immense and nearly empty space. She'd found many crates of long expired survival rations, a half dozen thin blankets and an austere portable space commode.

When she heard the First Mate clattering and bellowing his way down the passageway, Jana hurried back to the spot near the hatch where Boz had left her.

The door creaked open and the unruly pirate flung Ramesh into the compartment. The battered grad student was encrusted with dried blood, his left eye was swollen shut and a long ragged gash ran across his forehead.

The unlucky janitor and student intern tumbled into the chamber. Although apparently unharmed, both men shared the same expression of utter terror.

Finally Boz hurled Erik through the hatchway. Her deranged assistant was tightly bound with a thick scratchy rope. Hideous red welts from the restraints covered much of his nearly naked body. He quivered and shrieked at the rough treatment as a wild animal might under similar conditions.

The ruthless First Mate joined the novice slaves; "You will begin work in the morning." He grinned scornfully at Ramesh, "As you can see, any misbehavior will be repaid with harsh treatment."

Boz beckoned to the cabin boy and the two pirates left the miserable group in the locked compartment.

● ● ●

The trio aboard the *Seiran* was crowded into the snug cockpit admiring Mars as the ship streaked across the orbit of the red planet at over 45 AU/yr.

Ryo had insisted that his young charges should take time off from their various routines to celebrate the event.

Lev grumbled that the 'trivial occasion' cut into the time that he would spend on his painstaking examination of the records of the *Butin Belle*. Keira had been equally cranky beforehand, maintaining that she should skip the group meeting and continue to familiarize herself with the *Seiran's* copious weaponry.

128

But the old Investigator knew better; after nearly eight days of tedium in the cramped interceptor with the oddly wary young people, he felt that the group would function much better following the short diversion of the Mars crossing.

From below the sturdy external umbrella of the ship's forward facing Cosmic Ray deflector, Ryo watched as Keira huddled next to Lev for an optimal view as the man pressed himself against the window in awe.

"It's really amazing," Lev whispered.

The tiny and scattered lights from the Martian outposts bejeweled the nightside surface of the planet.

"I've been there twice," Keira uttered as she gawked at the dusky orb, "once when I was three and again when I was about eight."

The tawny sphere rapidly receded.

Ryo studied the spectacle from behind their overlapping shoulders.

"The only two things that I remember about Mars," Keira recalled nostalgically, "was jumping around like a little kangaroo in the low gravity and the fine red dust that was everywhere." She laughed at the childhood memories; "It took weeks to clean it out of everything when we got back to Free City."

Lev shook his head in envy, "I've never been there."

"Twenty years ago," Ryo reminisced, "when I was an Investigator Fourth Class, I was sent along with a big group from the Inquisitor's Office to look into irregularities at the Eos Mensa Cobalt Mine. That, I'm afraid to say, was my only trip to the red planet."

• • •

Jana had spent hours tending to Ramesh and Erik's wounds in the cavernous cargo compartment.

She and her coworkers had talked almost nonstop since Boz had imprisoned them together. Jana finally learned that the janitor's name was Lucas. The man was especially worried about his wife and young daughter who had lived in one of the small apartments at the Lunar Lab. She didn't have the heart to tell the poor soul that his family had quite certainly been killed by the blast that destroyed the facility.

The pudgy student intern was named Philip; he was a bright fifteen year old on his first trip away from home. If he ever saw his parents again, the teenager would have nearly unbelievable traveler's tales to share with them.

Philip and Lucas told her about the terrible abuse that Ramesh had suffered since the *Lightning* had arrived. Both Bosco and Captain Gristle had taken great efforts to beat the sometimes-arrogant and often defiant man.

Jana listened in alarm as the men described Erik's rapid and unexplainable descent into madness shortly after the pirates had snatched them from the Moon.

All were starved.

The slaves greedily devoured dozens of the moldering rations. Although eventually satiated by the substandard fare, Jana felt quite queasy after the rancid feast.

They slept fitfully heaped together, loosely bound against the lack of gravity by the rope that had constrained Erik.

When they heard the approaching pirates in the passageway, the five slaves trembled and groaned uncontrollably in despair.

• • •

The respite during the Mars crossing earlier in the day had paid off, Ryo noted as he pulled himself through the dark narrow passageway towards the cockpit. For the first time in weeks, his shipmates had spent much of the day together as they worked through their various tasks. As he had returned from the lavatory, he'd glimpsed Keira and Lev clenched in a passionate embrace in the dim sleeping berth of the *Seiran*.

Thankfully the sexual tension and the inexplicable animosity between the two was now likely to vanish.

Ryo smiled smugly as he slipped into the pilot's seat for the second half of the midnight watch; to his surprise, he rather enjoyed his burgeoning role as the group's patriarch. Perhaps he would expand upon the notion when he returned to Free City.

The old Investigator's mirthful contemplation was interrupted when the incoming message light flashed several times.

Ryo studied the sender information; the dispatch was from Carla Stuhr.

He watched the recorded message that she had sent hours earlier, *"I've just discovered another unusual ripple."*

The shadowy image of the woman glanced at the

desktop display, *"It's much smaller than the earlier one."*

She made several adjustments to the bright image before continuing; *"It's a single small very dense object with a mass of about 1,200 grams traveling at around 75 kilometers per second."*

Carla stared at him in concern, *"I don't have a very good plot on the trajectory yet, but it seems to have originated near Lutetia and is headed towards Earth!"*

20. News Item:
The war of words continues

Dateline: 30th of July, 2445; Arusha, EurAfrica, Earth

The bitter rancor continues to escalate between Daniel Kufuzu, the Exalted Warlord of EurAfrica and his much younger half-brother, Dimitri Verhovnyi, the Supreme Imperial Warlord of the Outer Reaches.

The current war of words was set off many years ago when Verhovnyi claimed that Kufuzu had attempted to clandestinely derail the construction of his immense Kuiper Belt Gas Refinement Facility. The Free City Inquisitor's Office has since determined that, in fact, Kufuzu had secretly meddled with the establishment of the facility because it would eventually out produce the Xenon gas monopoly of the EurAfrican Exotic Gas Consortium of which he is the primary stakeholder.

In the current wave of acrimony, Kufuzu accused Verhovnyi of complicity in the assassination of his third wife, Sophia, as she attended trade talks in New Rome. The still unexplained murder in late May has continued to baffle New Roman investigators.

Speaking from the capital city of Arusha yesterday, the EurAfrican Warlord promised brutal retaliation against his brother if he is implicated in the crime.

Verhovnyi for his part accused Kufuzu of using the assassination of his wife to fan the growing anti Outer Reaches sentiment on Earth. The Warlord of the Outer Reaches even went so far as to imply that his brother may have had a hand in the woman's murder.

Dimitri Verhovnyi luridly proclaimed in a press release from the Outer Reaches that "death would soon rain down upon Kufuzu for his treacherous misdeeds."

21. The plummeting sky

The Spanish teenager shivered as he crawled out of the warm little backpacker's tent. It was a surprisingly cold evening for equatorial East Africa.

He smiled to himself as he stood up; the chilly air probably had much more to do with elevation than anything else. After all, at nearly 4,600 meters above sea level, he could easily have expected a light dusting of snow on Mount Meru.

He switched on his lamp and studied the tiny campsite. The little ravine that he'd hastily chosen earlier after the bleary all day solo hike from the outfitter's base camp now seemed ideal after a much needed nap. The steep cliffs of gray volcanic rubble that surrounded the tent shielded his flimsy abode from the ever-present wind that buffeted the peak.

Overhead, thousands of glinting stars populated the indigo sky. He checked the time, it would take about twenty minutes to hike to the vantage point and witness the spectacular view far below on the Maasai Steppes that he'd come all this way to see.

He closed the flap of the tent and started off.

He'd left the stodgy comfort of his parent's home in Madrid nearly six months ago as a naive seventeen-year-old, full of himself and the unattainable ideals of the Enlightenment Crusade. His new Crusade "friends" had robbed and abandoned him after a long, slow train ride together to New Rome. He had reluctantly contacted his parents for help after only eleven days on the road. His father had grudgingly sent him five hundred Units and indicated that no more would be forthcoming should other disasters arise.

The experience had left him much more wary of entanglements. He'd met two beautiful young women on the Mediterranean crossing. Both seemed mildly interested in him, but they were bound for a western Morocco beach enclave and he for the Great Rift Valley. After a long night of drinking together in Tunis, they'd split up.

He'd wandered eastward alone across North Africa to Egypt before arriving at the Nile and the ruins of the ancient city of Cairo. He'd lived with an ever-changing group of like-minded vagabonds in a squatter's camp outside of Memphis for nearly a month. On his eighteenth birthday, he'd set out for the Rift Valley far to the south. He told his casual companions at the camp that he planned to scale at least three of East Africa's tallest mountains before his next birthday.

The Ripple In Space-Time

After much effort, he had arrived in Nairobi and several days later ventured to the top of Mount Kilimanjaro. But Africa's highest peak had been a disappointment. The towering volcano was an unsatisfying tourist trap catering to rich and flabby tourists and curio hunters. More than once on the tame and well-paved trail up the mountain, street vendors had offered him "Kilimanjaro Kocktails" or flimsy volcano snow globes.

At the crowded peak, a young and athletic couple from New Reykjavik had suggested Mount Meru as a much more challenging and solitary undertaking.

Days later on the trip to Arusha, he had met an ancient black man who professed to be the descendant of Maasai warriors that had stalked lions around the banks of the Mara River before it was channelized and diverted for agricultural purposes in 2280. The old man had claimed to have seen huge herds of zebra and gazelle trailed by a few vigilant big cats north of the bustling capital city. When he scoffed at the man's tale, the elderly African produced a tattered travel brochure as proof of the elaborate reforestation and "reanimalization" projects initiated by the EurAfrican government a few years earlier.

The old man had left him on the outskirts of the opulent capital city, mumbling something about great swarms of animals returning to the Maasai Steppes when, at last, the human hindrances had been seared away.

He shook his head and chuckled as he thought of the old African while he hiked in the cold blustery night air. Ahead was the outcropping that had been described to him earlier. He carefully scaled the craggy face of the dark edifice.

And there it was spread out below him.

Millions of lights from Arusha shimmered across the lowlands and oddly mimicked the droves of stalwart stars above. The immense and orderly arrangement of street lamps split the metropolis into tiny squares and rectangles each filled with dozens of wavering building lights. Long streams of headlights seeped down the main thoroughfares, conveying work-weary Africans back home.

At the horizon far to the southwest, the lights of the megacity merged with the star-splattered tapestry of the night sky. The cool and dispassionate celestial vista above was tremendously older than the cheery and emotional earth-bound construct below.

No doubt, he mused, his ancient ancestors had also marveled at the vast overhead realm many millennia before.

The Ripple In Space-Time

Slowly moving ruby or emerald lights plied purposefully through the star field, most likely satellites and space freighters, he realized.

As many teenagers had done before him, he contemplated his own insignificance compared to the nearly boundless cosmos that stretched out above. The cold windy air seemed to sharpen the reality of one's place in the grand scheme.

His philosophical introspection was interrupted by a peculiar sputtering orange speck high in the western sky.

Something was plummeting from above.

The smoldering ember grew steadily brighter as it arced down towards the steppes.

It seemed to be a large falling star, perhaps a meteor or a bit of space junk burning up in the atmosphere.

He hastily plotted the path of the heavenly invader, it seemed destined to impact the capital city he concluded in sudden panic.

With growing fear he followed the hurtling fireball.

The Spanish teenager cringed when the tumbling incandescent object exploded into scorching white light just above the city.

An angry and seething bubble of ultra hot gases expanded rapidly outward over the Maasai steppes and blasted against the base of the staunch peak.

The ensuing torrent of trillions of high energy gamma rays swiftly dispatched the lone backpacker perched on the high vantage point of Mount Meru.

Twenty-five seconds later the shock wave from the terrible blast tore his lifeless body apart.

22. News Item:
ARUSHA DESTROYED!

Dateline: 2nd of August, 2445; Nairobi, EurAfrica, Earth

The EurAfrican capital of Arusha is no more!

A tremendous explosion destroyed the city and severely damaged most of the neighboring suburbs last night. The city of Arusha and its nearly nine million residents were utterly wiped out by the blast.

Several badly injured survivors have reported seeing an odd shooting star plunging towards the doomed metropolis seconds before the destruction.

New Roman and Free City investigators are racing to the scene of the catastrophe. The Warlord Syndicate has pledged to aid any survivors.

Many in East Africa are already blaming Dimitri Verhovnyi and Outer Reaches terrorists for the horrific devastation.

Amidst the chaos of the disaster, this much is certain: at 9:23 pm local time, a tremendous aerial explosion destroyed the EurAfrican capital city.

After carefully scrutinizing all available information, scientists at the University of Nairobi released some preliminary data about the dreadful event. At about 550 meters above the spires of the opulent city, a magnetic containment bubble that had apparently contained slightly more than 500 grams of antimatter ruptured. The almost instantaneous annihilation of the small mass released nearly 90 petajoules of energy producing an immense explosion similar in size to a large old-style nuclear bomb.

The origin of the antimatter that destroyed the city is uncertain, however Dr. Hekima from the University of Nairobi noted that the radiation signature emanating from the strange shooting star that preceded the blast was remarkably similar to a small sample of anti-tauons that he had recently obtained from the late Dr. Jana Fesai of the Lunar Ultra Energy Research Laboratory.

Those who wish to contribute to the relief effort may make donations to the Free City Aid Society.

23. Calamity

No one had left the Student Union, Desiree suddenly realized, even though the meeting had jerked to a halt hours ago when they had first learned of the calamity.

Her head throbbed with a headache that felt as if thin, sharp knives were being jammed repeatedly into her skull. Her eyes were dry and itchy; she and nearly everyone else in the room had run out of tears long ago.

The video loop of the explosion began again, she'd seen it countless times already but she could *not* turn away.

The unfathomable disaster in East Africa had caused her poor little sister, Sabra to curl up on the floor next to her, shaking and whimpering like so many others in the meeting room.

Hours ago, many had wondered out loud as to who would have done this horrific deed. Now the weary and dumbstruck group endlessly endured the traumatic reoccurring communal nightmare that the video loop had come to signify.

Desiree stared at the video screen and steeled herself again for the replay of the atrocity that had repeated every twenty-seven seconds for many hours.

From high above and a bit to the north, an East African weather satellite had, by chance, recorded the disaster before the immense flash of the explosion had blinded the indifferent robotic observer.

A few thin clouds hovered to the south above the plains when a tiny red dot appeared at the left edge of the screen. The celestial visitor slowly moved about a quarter of the way across the screen before suddenly dropping out of orbit and racing downward towards the doomed city.

Desiree flinched just as the red speck reached the center of the metropolis. A rapidly spreading circle of white mercilessly consumed the city almost instantly before the satellite camera failed.

And it was over.

She had no idea when she would be able to summon some tiny reserve of inner strength to stagger out of the meeting room and bring an end to the unremitting ordeal.

The video loop restarted.

• • •

The radiation meter was still off the scale.

Constable Jones stared grimly out of the thick bulletproof viewport of the antique Armored Personnel Carrier as he drove slowly through the carnage. A sullen and moody red sun was just rising over the scorching dusty gray ruins of the Arushan Outer District neighborhood.

He had been trained to use the heavy old vehicle years ago should disasters arise in the capital city. His superiors had surmised then that riots, or much less likely, a volcanic eruption might someday menace the megacity.

But he knew this was neither.

His latest crew of five ragtag volunteer rescuers sat quietly behind him, likely all contemplating their certain impending demise. An hour earlier at the comparative safety of the Armory, they had watched in stunned silence when he returned with the previous crew of mortally radiation-sickened rescuers and, by then, the three expired 'survivors' that had been pried out of the wreckage.

Everyone seemed to sense the futility of the rescue operation, but the radiation levels were so high that any attempt to escape by fleeing would certainly be fatal as well.

In a strange twist of luck he had survived the blast because he had forgotten to salute his Commander when the pompous old fool had unexpectedly stopped by his office in the early evening. As punishment for his minor lapse in protocol, the old man had ordered him to stay late and tend to some filing in the basement Records Room. Although the building had collapsed around him, he'd managed to crawl out.

He'd been the only survivor at the district headquarters and had since put himself in charge of the hopeless rescue effort. Like most of the residents of Arusha, he was merely a scrf; his life meant nothing.

Three trips earlier, he'd spotted a few ghastly looking victims staggering around what he presumed was the site of the tourist hotel. The crew had spent twenty minutes collecting the survivors and loading them into the vehicle while he waited inside. When they reached the Armory, the rescuers were nearly indistinguishable from the victims.

Unquestionably he too would soon suffer the same fate.

• • •

"This will lead to riots," Chief Inspector Helga Bennet muttered to herself as she sat alone in her somber darkened office.

She undoubtedly held the dubious honor of being the first person in Free City to learn of the catastrophe.

It had all started hours ago, while she was engaged in a heated late evening conference call with Inspector Second Class Zara Kamchatka in Nairobi and Liaison Agent Hugo Mackillroy in New Rome regarding the investigation into the assassination of Madame Kufuzu.

Mac had definitely linked the murder to some sort of plot that was a foot to kill the Warlord of EurAfrica. He and Zara had been arguing about who would track down a few feeble leads in Arusha when it happened.

Helga had recalled that the image on her desktop screen of the wilily woman Inspector in East Africa had strangely flicked and briefly faded before returning to normal. When the unusual communication anomaly had passed, Zara had an uncommon look of terror.

"There was a flash and now the ground is shaking!" she'd yelled before fleeing.

While Zara was escaping from the trembling building in Nairobi, Mac had quickly checked the seismic and satellite information for East Africa and relayed his findings that indeed some sort of huge blast had occurred in neighboring Arusha.

Helga had notified the Prime Minister of the disaster shortly afterwards and set about shifting through all available details. Information quickly surfaced about the extremely high radiation levels near the blast. Helga sent Zara to the University of Nairobi and a High Energy Physics Professor there confirmed her fears that most likely stolen antimatter from the Lunar Lab was to blame for the destruction of the EurAfrican capital.

In the ensuing hours, Helga had talked to dozens of Inspectors and Agents on Earth and elsewhere; all reported the horrified shock and revulsion of the locals upon learning of the sneak attack.

Disturbingly, several incidences of vandalism and vicious vigilantly justice had already surfaced in outlying areas.

24. News Item:
Sabbatical for beloved professor

Dateline: 3rd of August, 2445; Free City University, Free City, Earth

Free City University's much-idolized Professor Malcolm Evans of the Department of Advanced Applied Molecular Biology unexpectedly announced today that he would begin an unscheduled sabbatical effective immediately.

The revered instructor revealed that he and two associates would be tending to an unusual and pressing new opportunity at an undisclosed research site in the remote Trojan Asteroid Field.

School of Biology officials wished Professor Evans well in his upcoming endeavor and announced that Professor Suzuki would take over his teaching responsibilities for the rest of the academic year.

Classes will proceed as normal beginning next week.

25. Extortion

"My requirements are modest, for now," the fuzzy video image of Dimitri Verhovnyi continued, "I must receive a good faith payment of one million Standard Units from each of the six fiefdoms by midnight Titan time or I shall let loose further destruction."

Ryo paused the recording that Helga had forwarded to the *Seiran* and studied his horrified crewmates. "The message is three days old."

Keira stared at the old Investigator in panic, "Did everyone pay him off in time?"

"Fortunately yes." Ryo glared at the frozen image of the madman, "EurAfrica was the only fiefdom that didn't comply immediately; mainly because the capital city is in ruins. To stave off potential bombardment, the New Roman City Council sent the bribe for their entire fiefdom."

He rubbed his forehead in dismay, "Helga said that the Free City Municipal government sent an offering as well, apparently to avoid any ambiguities that could lead to the fair city's demise."

Lev's head slumped onto Keira's shoulder. He

had barely spoken since they had learned of the catastrophe that had claimed the jewel of EurAfrica.

Ryo sighed, "I'm sorry to say that there is more." He restarted the recording.

The Outer Reaches Warlord sneered, "If anyone should foolishly attempt to circumvent my wishes or harm me in any way, dozens of these devices will rain upon the fiefdoms in a most malicious torrent of death."

The message ended abruptly.

"Could he really have so many weapons?" Keira asked.

Lev shook his head, "No, judging by Carla's original Gravitational observations, probably only 3 or 4 of the Tau blockbusters."

Ryo nodded in agreement.

"But," Lev added ominously, "he may have plenty of the more common and difficult to detect standard matter/antimatter weapons that were leftover from the Second Amero-Asian War."

Ryo stared pensively out at the rubbly vastness of the Asteroid Belt, "I'm afraid that this puts an especially keen edge on our hunt for the pirates and the *Butin Belle*."

"Right now, we're the only people who could put an end to this madness."

• • •

"Son of a bitch!" Olin Gristle protested loudly when the message light on the control panel of the *Butin Belle* began to blink again. "How many friggin' times is he going to check up on us?"

Fortunately due to the time delay of many hours, the nagging Warlord could not communicate directly with Captain Gristle.

Olin steadied himself and viewed the latest of the eight messages that Dimitri Verhovnyi had sent in the past dozen hours.

"Gristle, I need those devices now!" the Warlord shouted in panic. "If someone discovers that I'm bluffing..." his voice trailed off in despair. Dimitri forced an uneasy smile, "Let me know as soon as they're ready."

The Captain shook his head in contempt, if the Shipjacks had managed to get the *Lightning* to the rendezvous in the Asteroid Belt on time then his slaves from the lunar lab would have had more than enough time to build Dimitri's weapons.

After several seconds of irritation, Gristle deleted the message. He wouldn't even bother to look in on Boz and the slaves on the *Lightning*.

Persistent pestering on behalf of their jittery employer would not go well with his recalcitrant First Mate.

• • •

"Yes, Prime Minister," Chief Inspector Helga Bennet assured the head of the Free City government at the hastily arranged meeting, "the Inquisitor's Office is tracking down the explosives."

The venerable leader nodded, "We have a second group attempting to covertly stop Dimitri Verhovnyi."

Helga's bushy eyebrows arched up, "The CRAMP, I assume."

"Indeed; we've loaned them a particularly fast prototype interceptor spacecraft." The Prime Minister winced, "Let's hope they are successful."

• • •

"With the receipt of the good faith payments, all have avoided destruction for now," Dimitri

154

derided as he began recording his second proclamation.

"Each fiefdom must now send an official delegation to the Titan Palace to pay tribute to my elevated status as the Supreme Exalted Ruler of All Humanity."

He smiled menacingly, "Fiefdoms that fail to deliver suitable offerings and envoys shall risk punishment."

The door to his chamber creaked open.

Dimitri frowned, his concentration on the extravagant demands had been broken. The Warlord of the Outer Reaches, recently self-appointed as Supreme Exalted Ruler of All Humanity swiveled around for the source of the unwelcome interruption.

His slave girl cowered at the door obviously aware of her unfortunate transgression.

"GET OUT!"

The heavy door slammed shut.

Dimitri fumed as he collected himself.

He restarted the recording, "With the receipt of the good faith payments..."

"You will work here," Boz pointed to the well-equipped maintenance compartment.

Jana nodded as she appraised the facility located off of the labyrinth of passageways somewhere in the huge robotic space tanker. "Where do we get parts and supplies?"

The First Mate spread his hands, "Scrounge whatever you want from this heap. We've got three and a half trillion Units of stolen hardware here that ain't never gonna be seen again." He smirked at his lone prisoner, "You and your friends will of course have a grouchy pirate or two tagging along when you hunt for parts."

"Naturally," Jana nodded.

They drifted into the workroom.

"What is it that you would like for us to build, Boz?"

The First Mate tapped on a wall mounted display screen and a see-through image of a small and sturdy looking sphere appeared.

Jana studied the image of the complex device for many minutes. She pointed at the tiny speck in the center of mechanism, "This is anti-tau iron."

"You're not as stupid as you look," the pirate mocked.

Just as Jana had feared, she and the others were now expected to create an unimaginably destructive miniature weapon. "Where are we going to find tau iron?"

"We brought it all with us from the moon lab, sweetheart," he gloated.

• • •

The trio onboard the *Seiran* had spent twelve grueling hours scanning the miniscule sector of the Asteroid Belt for any signs of gravitational abnormalities and the elusive *Butin Belle*.

Ryo looked up hopefully at Keira as she concentrated on the wide sweep radar screen. "Anything?"

She shook her head in dismay.

"Lev?" the old Inspector called back to the young man awkwardly pressed into the tightly packed gravitational survey compartment that had been hastily added to the ship.

"Nothing."

Ryo slumped in defeat. All of humanity depended on their uncertain luck in locating and

157

stopping the fugitives and hopefully retrieving the stolen antimatter.

Keira stared at him sympathetically. "If I was going to hide out from the law," she pointed at the vast and slowly tumbling multitude of mountain-sized boulders that stretched out beyond the porthole, "I'd do it out there."

26. News Item:
Megalomaniac of the Outer Reaches

Dateline: 8th of August, 2445; Vesta, The
Asteroid Belt and Jupiter Colonies

With the heinous obliteration of Arusha and the
unforgivable slaughter of so many Africans only
a week ago, the fury of the inhabitants of Vesta
in the Asteroid Belt and Jupiter Colonies has
risen to a most vindictive level.

Scores of angry miners ransacked the local
headquarters of the Outer Reaches Trade
Representative last night, killing two scummy
henchmen of the villainous Warlord who were
unfortunate enough to be in the offices at the
time of the riot.

Indifferent Vestan police officers watched the
mob carry out the lawless deeds. Several
patrolmen reportedly loaned their weapons to the
miners to aid in the summary justice.

Many of the rioters vowed to take up arms and
storm the far off Titan Palace with the hopes of
casting off the tight new noose of tyranny that
has recently slipped around the neck of
humanity.

The Ripple In Space-Time

Others dealt with the prospect of the unstable megalomaniac in different ways.

It was widely reported yesterday that the citizenry of several cities on Earth and Mars carried out silent mass demonstrations. Most of these events were meant to mourn for the tremendous loss of life, but a few had a more pathetic purpose, that of preparing the residents for the grim likelihood of a long subjugation by the barbaric overlord.

The Prime Minister's Office in Free City promised to comply with Dimitri Verhovnyi's lurid demands. Most residents of the metropolis however view that cooperation as a vile and cowardly form of capitulation. A noisy demonstration led by Enlightenment Crusaders flared up at the University. The young ne'er-do-wells bemoaned the tragic turn of events as further evidence of the steady decline of the human species.

New Roman authorities for their part have skittishly succumbed to the madman's ever-escalating ultimatums. At least six large freighters will shortly depart from low Earth orbit bound for the Titan Palace loaded with expensive offerings for the illegitimate despot.

Meanwhile the search and rescue work continues in the vast radioactive dustbin that was once Arusha.

160

27. Tensions abound

"Just stay away from me!" Keira flared.

Lev hastily retreated from the sleeping berth and scurried towards the neutral area of the cockpit where Ryo was busy with the seemingly endless search.

The young man slumped into the Second Mate's seat and glanced warily back down the passageway towards the apparently now forbidden compartment.

The old Investigator studied his perplexed cohort.

"It was going so well," Lev shook his head in dismay, "I don't know what happened."

"Just leave her alone for a few days," Ryo muttered. "We've all been working far too hard for the last week on this hunt. I know it seems that we'll be stuck together in this tiny ship forever."

Lev rubbed his forehead in frustration and stared at the wide sweep radar display, "I hope you're right."

• • •

The Ripple In Space-Time

Boz idly watched her work from across the Maintenance Compartment.

Ramesh had proved to be less than worthless, Jana groused as she struggled to wire the magnetic field generator into the tiny sphere.

While she and the two other able-bodied slaves labored nearly continuously to produce the miniature weapons for their impatient and frequently abusive capturers, Ramesh stayed behind in the aft cargo bay with Erik. When he did accompany them to the maintenance compartment, he often haphazardly tampered with the three unfinished devices.

Boz had beaten Ramesh twice in the workshop for his blunders. Now the pirates seemed to prefer that the troublesome grad student remain behind in the cargo compartment.

With luck, Jana realized with some trepidation, she could soon load the finicky antimatter cores into the weapons. She still had unanswered questions as to who had produced the design work for the complex devices; certainly not the pirates nor their mysterious employer.

No, she realized with a start, this was the work of a clever Advanced Physicist; probably someone that she knew.

The hatch creaked open.

162

Jana smiled briefly when the two slaves returned with the tattered old pirate who had watched over them as they scavenged parts elsewhere on the *Lightning*. Philip held up several vector compilers and Lucas showed off a thick coil of red-sheathed wire.

She nodded her encouragement and the men set the supplies aside.

Both Philip and Lucas had proven to be excellent technicians, producing far better work than the much more experienced Ramesh.

Boz methodically searched the men for contraband.

Jana watched the routine pat down with frustration, with the First Mate's persistent vigilance, she might never have an opportunity to sabotage the three weapons.

• • •

For several seconds Ryo stared in disbelief at the flashing red incoming message light on the communication panel of the quiet cockpit. 'Red' meant someone nearby was attempting to contact them, he recalled doltishly as he contemplated the late night interruption.

He checked the particulars of the unprecedented dispatch; it was a heavily encoded live audio message marked 'Top Secret for Inspector Trop Only. Biometric Validation Required.'

Who would know that he was loitering around in the *Seiran* in this obscure sector?

Ryo studied the radar for several seconds: nothing. Apparently the sender was well disguised.

The flashing red light continued to beckon.

He pressed the acknowledge button and slid his fingertips over the interface panel to confirm his identity.

After several seconds, an eerie fluttering hum caused by the profuse encryption filled the cockpit.

"Ryo? Ryo Trop?"

"Trop here. Who is this?"

"Zmuda. Are you alone?"

The old Inspector checked down the passageway. Lev was apparently still asleep in the improvised bunk that he'd cobbled together in the cargo compartment while Keira was slumbering alone in the coveted berth.

"Go ahead Lieutenant."

"Excellent! We're about three thousand kilometers above you right now traveling at just over 75 AU/yr!"

Ryo noticed a delay of about two seconds. "How are you managing that speed?"

"Secret new technology. With Kufuzu's untimely death, the CRAMP has switched all its efforts to Dimitri Verhovnyi."

The lag time was already noticeably longer.

"A worthy target."

"You'll hear soon...that the Inquisitor's Office and the CRAMP...are working together to stop further carnage. Good...luck...with locating...the pirates...."

Zmuda was rapidly slipping out of range.

Ryo smiled at the good news, "Good luck to you too, Lieutenant."

• • •

After an especially nerve-racking day of loading the volatile antimatter into the three weapons, Jana was in no mood for the travails that were awaiting her when she and the others were rudely shoved back into the aft cargo compartment.

"NO! NO!" Erik screamed at Ramesh. "You tricked me! YOU TRICKED ME!"

The writhing madman flailed indiscriminately at the grad student.

Lucas and Philip seized Erik and pulled him away.

Jana pushed the grad student roughly back towards the outer bulkhead, "What the *hell* is going on here?"

"He tricked me!" Erik's voice echoed across the vast compartment.

Ramesh shook his badly scratched face, "It's nothing, don't listen to him."

"He had me design a tau antimatter weapon for him!" Erik shouted.

"What?" Jana stared in horrified disbelief at the grad student.

"He said he built a bomb at the Lab for the pirates!" Erik ranted.

"He's crazy. Months ago, I told him that I needed help with the research for my dissertation about massive particle annihilations and he put together a rendition of a sample device," Ramesh smiled disarmingly. "He *was* my Faculty Advisor, after all."

"The plans!" Her head pounded with the frightening implications of his apparent duplicity. "How did the friggin' pirates know about the plans!"

Ramesh had the terrified look of a mischievous child caught after a misdeed had gone terribly wrong. "I was...They were going to pay me," he stammered, "for the drawings and a working device... Then they stole both of them when they kidnaped us."

"Hundreds were killed," she growled like an enraged beast, "the lab was destroyed and we were abducted because you were bribed?"

Ramesh nodded with remorse.

She shook violently.

Again and again she bashed him against the unforgiving wall of the chamber.

When it was finally done, Jana hovered over his battered corpse still seething at his self-serving betrayal of humanity.

The hatch creaked open and Boz glared angrily at the disturbance in the compartment.

Lucas and Philip cowered far off to the side, both tightly restraining Erik who had watched the lethal pummeling with an odd sort of demented retribution.

The pirate floated across the cell to scrutinize the body.

"What happened here?"

"He fell and bumped his head," Jana said flatly.

In the zero gravity of the ship, Boz glanced at the bloody remains and laughed at the absurdity of her explanation.

"Nicely done," the First Mate jeered, "it would have been you or I who eventually did the deed, I'm sure."

• • •

"...and so those are the weapons systems," Keira appraised the old Investigator. "In short, we certainly could disable the *Butin Belle* with this firepower and probably completely destroy it, if need be."

Ryo nodded to the woman as they drifted back to the cockpit. Blasting willy-nilly at the ship would likely cause the cargo of antimatter to explode and vaporize them as well.

"What have you discovered about the *Seiran's* other abilities?"

They floated past the sleeping berth where Lev was loudly snoring.

"It was designed to be a very nimble ship. I'll show you a fascinating trick." She settled into the pilot's seat.

Ryo slipped into the copilot's chair next to her.

"This controls an anti-detection system that masks us by duplicating the background electromagnetic interference."

"Impressive."

"We should be able to get within a few hundred meters of the *Butin Belle* undetected."

"Good work, young lady," Ryo smiled. "Now tell me what's behind your current difficulties with Lev."

Her shoulders slumped visibly.

"I really like him," she whispered sheepishly, "but I just don't think that Lev will settle down and apply himself sufficiently to ever satisfy me."

He studied her crestfallen face.

"I think you're too hard on him. I know that he can be a bit eccentric and promiscuous at times, but he is a good guy."

"I know," she confessed. "I think he just reminds me of my far less than perfect parents: all pleasure and no pragmatism."

Ryo considered her for several seconds before continuing, "It's not always bad to have a little mischievous fun with those that happen to surround you."

She stared at him skeptically.

"It's true, my dear. I had a mate long ago," Ryo reminisced, "her name was Talya. We were married for a short time about thirty years ago."

"What happened?"

"I was a busy young Investigator working way too many hours and Talya finally gave up on me when she realized that I wasn't likely to ever spend those fleeting simple moments with her."

"That's sad."

"It was all the result of my own selfishness and shortsightedness," Ryo acknowledged, "that I lost someone that I'd hoped to live with forever."

The woman nodded as she contemplated her own recent intolerance towards Lev.

• • •

She felt surprisingly heroic.

Jana had, only twelve hours earlier, murdered a man and just now she had finally succeeded in very subtly sabotaging the three weapons.

Both had been ridiculously easy, Jana gloated with macabre gratification.

Several days ago she had deduced how to subvert the will of her capturers by depriving them of the devices and any future use of the hazardous tau antimatter, all without harming or casting blame on herself and the other slaves.

When Boz had unexpectedly left her in the maintenance compartment guarded only by the cabin boy, Jana had hastily attached the automatic destruct timers that she had secretly constructed earlier.

It was really quite simple; when the timers shut off the magnetic field that kept the tiny antimatter core safely separated from the ordinary matter casing, the antimatter would swiftly collide with the casing and the ensuing blast would vaporize everything within twenty kilometers.

She had rigged the timers to cycle every 48 hours; if she didn't reset them manually in that period, the weapons would explode. If her kidnappers launched the devices, they would surely self-destruct long before they could reach any target.

The final spiteful touch to the scheme was the tamper-proofing, Jana mused; any attempt to alter the timers without going through a complex and counterintuitive procedure would set off an explosion.

Boz returned with the others from a scavenging expedition. The cabin boy stared dumbly at the First Mate before departing the workroom.

The pirate drifted over to inspect the progress that she had made during the morning.

"What's that?" Boz pointed at the doomsday autotrigger.

"It's just the containment bubble timing cycler," Jana answered in a contrived huff.

"The first device that your dead friend made for us didn't have one," the pirate noted suspiciously.

"I'm sure it was smaller and much more sophisticated," she evaded.

Jana smiled disarmingly at the First Mate. "We've had to make do with the bits and pieces that the boys could find around the ship."

"Whatever works," Boz shrugged indifferently.

28. The tip

"The first thing that I'm going to do," Lev
wearily reported to his cohorts as they pulled
open the hatch of the *Seiran* and staggered into
the landing dock lobby of the Lutetia Asteroid
Mining Facility, "is to enjoy a hot shower."

That particular luxury, Ryo grumbled as he
inspected the austere outpost, was mostly likely
unavailable at any price.

Several unsavory regulars scattered around the
entryway studied the exhausted newcomers. Two
showed especially keen interest in Keira as the
trio trudged to the visitor's accommodations
check-in.

While they waited for an attendant, Lev laid his
head on the dusty countertop and dozed off,
Keira stood taciturn and transfixed in the dull
and utilitarian surroundings and Ryo drooped
achingly from the weeks of frustrating work.

For fifteen bleary days they had endured the
numbing tedium of the so far fruitless search for
the fugitives. When Ryo discovered Lev
repeatedly drifting off while monitoring the wide
sweep radar two days ago, the old Investigator
realized that his companions required a respite.

Ryo determined that the isolated mining station on Lutetia was the only acceptable facility in the vicinity and the *Seiran* diverted to the asteroid. As he studied the loitering locals, Ryo was now regretting the selection.

"Hi folks, it's good to see you." A heavily scared old man limped to the counter, "We don't often have visitors." He eyed the well-outfitted threesome, "At least visitors who aren't miners. Will you be staying the night?"

"Yes, three rooms for two nights," Keira answered for the exhausted travelers.

They had agreed beforehand that she would largely speak for the group in her role as a Liaison Officer. Ryo had gone to great lengths beforehand to conceal their identities and the true nature of their mission in the Asteroid Belt.

"That's quite a ship you have," the attendant noted as he studied the *Seiran* through the wide spaceport windows while the dockhands moored the sleek vessel.

Keira nodded halfheartedly, "We're doing some equipment endurance tests on this new model for the shipyard. It's really boring work."

She was carefully sticking to the story that they had repeatedly rehearsed before the landing.

"Way out here in the middle of nowhere?"

"Usually we run the tests near the Moon, but with all that's going on around Earth now, we're supposed to stay out of everyone's way."

"Well this is about as far out of everybody's way as you can get."

Ryo nudged Lev and the young man awoke from his impromptu nap.

"Three rooms for two nights," the attendant handed Keira a payment interface, "that'll be three hundred Units."

She forced a smile and slid her fingertips over the device, "*300 Standard Units charged to Victoria De Marchi of the Tranquility Shipyards.*"

"The rooms are just down the tunnel to the right. If you need anything, Vicky," the old man winked salaciously at Keira, "I'd be more than happy to help you out."

• • •

He felt much better, Ryo realized. Nearly twenty hours of sleep had certainly improved his disposition, although he was now ravenously hungry.

S F Chapman

The old Investigator wandered out of his minuscule room in search of food and his companions. The swing shift at the mine had apparently just ended and a mob of rowdy and rambunctious workers crowded into the complex from the maze of tunnels below.

After several minutes of bumping and jostling, he made his way to a lunchroom. The demure sign in the front of the workaday eatery suggested the preferred order of services to the patrons: *Cards and Food.*

While the regulars clustered around the card tables and buffet trays, Ryo studied the establishment. More than a few of the clientele apparently spent most of their money and surplus hours gambling at the well-worn blackjack tables.

He spotted Lev with two other greenhorns at a 'Three Unit Minimum' table in a glum corner of the crowded room. His cohort's dour expression advertised his lack of luck at the pastime. Ryo gestured to the man between hands and Lev nodded. The young man played one more round before giving up on any slim chance of retrieving his lost fortune.

Lev trudged over to an empty table and Ryo joined him with a plate of steamy and entirely too greasy food.

The Ripple In Space-Time

"How did you do at the card table?"

The young man grimaced, "Lost nearly six hundred Units."

Ryo tentatively prodded an unidentifiable brownish slab on his plate, "It won't be a problem." He sampled the dreadful fodder and wisely switched to a more promising pool of lumpy greenish goo, "Remember, 'Mr. Clawson' we have a full expense account for this endeavor."

After several seconds of bewilderment at the use of the unfamiliar name, Lev nodded knowingly, "Oh, that's right!"

"Where's Ms Di Marchi?"

"I think she's next door at the bar."

Lev pointed with alarm at an approaching group of boisterous miners.

Four burly locals crowded around the table with plates piled high with food.

An especially hefty fellow scowled at Ryo, "You two from Free City?"

"Yeah, but we haven't been there for months."

The big man softened a bit, "So you missed that
178

friggin' sneak attack on EurAfrica?"

"Fortunately, we were doing endurance testing on a new ship in the Belt when it happened."

The group of miners looked much more empathetic now.

"I have a cousin from Arusha," a scruffy old miner volunteered, "luckily she was in Nairobi on business when it happened."

"I heard from a friend," Ryo added, "that everyone is worried that they'll be next if Dimitri Verhovnyi doesn't get his way."

"Most of my relatives were wiped out long ago in the war," a young man interjected, "I don't want anything like that to happen again."

"For once I'm glad that nobody knows that we are here on Lutetia," the lanky man at the far end of the table voiced what was probably the sentiments of most of the residents of the mining facility.

The others reluctantly agreed.

"How's it been here since the blast?" the Investigator fished around for information.

"Production in the mine is way up," the big man groused. "Nobody can figure out if it's just to

179

keep us busy or if the mine owners are stockpiling ore to take advantage of any spike in metal prices due to war."

"Some of the new guys wanna storm the Palace on Titan and kill that friggin' bastard," the young workman growled.

The older miners chuckled at the rough and ready novice.

"When they sent us out to the Belt," Lev said warily, "they warned us about pirates. Is there any of that stuff going on around here?"

"No," the scruffy old man said, "they pretty much stay away from Lutetia. I guess the goons in the Mining Guild scare them off."

Ryo pushed the littered plate aside, he'd finished as much of the atrocious meal as he could endure. "It's been nice to meet you gentlemen, but sadly we have to get back to work ourselves."

• • •

They spotted Keira a few minutes later chit-chatting with a fawning group of roustabouts in a gloomy bar ironically called the *Parisian*.

As they slipped into a nearby booth, Ryo noticed Lev staring jealously at the flirtatious crowd of drunken men.

After several minutes of giggly interplay with the laborers, Keira pointed to the booth and strolled over.

"Who are those guys?" Ryo asked Keira.

"Most of them independently mine the surrounding asteroids." She shook her head sympathetically, "They tell me that it's brutal work."

Several of the inebriated workers waved to Keira from across the room. Lev frowned at the attention that the woman elicited from the motley men.

Ryo glanced at the group, "Since you were trained as a liaison to the locals, see what you can find out about our fugitives."

Keira smiled pleasantly at the old Investigator before rejoining the workmen.

"We've only have about a half a day left before we have to resume the search," Ryo mentioned to Lev as his sidekick grimly watched over the woman.

The young man rubbed his head in exacerbation, "Yeah."

The Ripple In Space-Time

"When we're all locked up in the *Seiran* again," the old Investigator warned his unhappy colleague, "I want you to really work at getting along with her."

Lev stared miserably at his mentor.

"Remember that we're not at the Free City University Student Union here where you can hop in and out of bed with no great consequences. When the time comes, the three of us must work together flawlessly or we could well perish as squabbling fools."

Keira returned to the booth with her arm wrapped around a roughhewn youngster who looked barely fifteen.

"Go ahead, Benny," she coaxed the teenager, "tell my boss about what you spotted the other day."

The wide-eyed newcomer studied Ryo before beginning, "I was heading back here yesterday from Rock 853111, which is a dinky asteroid about four days away that my brothers and I are secretly mining."

The kid cautiously scanned the surrounding patrons for eavesdroppers before continuing, "I gotta be really careful when I bring in a load of ore so that the Mining Guild doesn't find out what we're doing."

Ryo nodded reassuringly at the implied subterfuge.

Keira stroked the teen's hand to fortify his waning confidence.

"I had the wide sweep radar set on 'high' and I picked up something lurking way off in the distance. I thought it might be a Guild Interceptor."

Lev tipped his head in interest at the tidbit, "What was it?"

"I couldn't see anything, so I finally used the telescope. Even then, I could barely make it out."

"Tell them what you think it was, Benny," Keira prompted.

"I'm pretty sure that it was that big tanker that got hijacked awhile ago in the Outer Reaches."

"The *Xenon Lightning*?" Ryo asked skeptically.

"Yeah, that's the one."

"Was it adrift?" Lev inquired.

The youngster shook his head.

"Interesting; why would a particularly valuable commandeered gas transport be out here?" Ryo

183

wondered.

Keira kissed the kid's cheek in appreciation, "See Benny; I told you that they'd like your story."

29. The risky ruse

It had taken hours and no small amount of luck for Lieutenant Zmuda to finally 'lock' the stealthy vessel into an oddly skewed orbit around Saturn that would conceal it from detection by any observers on Titan.

The crew was still stiff and disoriented from the blisteringly fast trip that had required their prolonged confinement to acceleration couches in the diminutive vehicle.

"Well, you two certainly look the part," Mixion noted as she helped Jasper and the Lieutenant into their disguises as they prepared for the risky first encounter with the unstable Warlord in the Titan Palace.

The men reluctantly climbed through the docking port and sealed the heavy hatch.

A dozen minutes later, the shrewd young woman watched though the porthole as they rocketed away in the tiny landing craft towards the huge unseen moon.

Her part in the imperative assassination attempt would not arrive for many days and would depend entirely on their slim chances of success.

"You may see the Supreme Exalted Ruler of All Humanity now," the stern palace guard reported to the men.

After enduring two very thorough searches for hidden weapons and spending hours in a waiting room that would have been flatteringly called a jail cell anywhere else, Jasper and Lieutenant Zmuda finally followed the sentry to the Warlord's chamber.

"Please remember that all visitors to the Palace are carefully watched at all times," the guard mentioned.

The heavily armed sentinel paused at the door, "Gentlemen, be sure to bow when you meet the Warlord. You must refer to him only as the Supreme Exalted Ruler." He knocked tentatively on the door. "If you displease him, you risk execution."

Jasper frowned at the severe edict.

The guard pushed open the door, "Oh my Master, the Supreme Exalted Ruler of All Humanity; two provisions traffickers wish to converse with you on a matter of commerce."

Zmuda suppressed a sneer when he first caught sight of the most reviled of all men.

Dimitri waved the visitors into the room without looking up from the mounds of work spread around his worktable, "I have no need for whatever overpriced supplies you two are hawking."

The men respectfully lowered their heads.

"Oh Super Exalted Leader," Jasper twanged in his thick Australian accent.

Dimitri scowled at the minor gaffe.

"We've come to buy, not sell."

A smug grin darted across the Warlord's face, "Well then, that is a different matter."

Zmuda extended his hand, "My business associate and I operate a modest trading vessel. We make a long slow circuit between the Kuiper Belt Station at one end and the Eros Asteroid Encampment at the other."

Just as the two clandestine assassins had predicted, Dimitri's unquenchable impulse to strike a bargain was obvious.

"What is it that you desire, my friends?"

"Our ship is small and the journey is long," Jasper lamented. "My shipmate has a nimble young drudge to see to his manly wishes, but I currently have none."

Zmuda nodded lecherously, "We happened upon a Slaver at a watering hole on Vesta who said that you were in possession of an underage girl that you planned to sell off soon."

The Warlord beamed at his luck. "Perhaps I could part with the dear thing," his eyebrows arched up in fake sentiment, "although she's just like a daughter to me."

"Naturally," Jasper turned towards the door, "we wouldn't dream of separating you from the beloved tyke."

"But," Dimitri held up his hand, "although she's grown a bit too old to be a submissive parlormaid, I suspect that the wretch would be superbly acquiescent to your perverted requirements."

"Excellent," Zmuda cooed.

"May we inspect the cherub?" Jasper asked.

Dimitri nodded, "GIRL!"

The door creaked open.

A particularly spindly child with huge sad eyes stood shivering at the portal, "Yes Master?"

"Come here."

The girl complied.

The Warlord smoothed her rumpled brown hair. "Turn around, let us have a good look at you."

Her head drooped in shame as the three men stared ominously.

"I suppose she'll do," Jasper frowned.

Zmuda nodded.

"There is one little matter that I'd like to assure myself of in private, if I may," Jasper smiled at the Warlord.

"Of course," Dimitri acknowledged. "Girl, take this trader to the slave quarters and obey him as if he were your Master."

The poor parlormaid had a look of overwhelming panic at the unprecedented request, "Yes sir."

Zmuda and Dimitri watched the child usher the big man away.

When the door closed, Zmuda turned to the Warlord, "He's rather well-endowed. I'm sure that he'd like to measure the merchandise for himself."

"Shall we discuss the price?" the Warlord asked greedily.

• • •

The little parlormaid led Jasper past the palace guard standing watchfully at the chamber door and down a short dim passageway to a filthy and dank cell littered with the cast off scraps that the pitiful child had collected over many years.

Jasper carefully inspected the tiny room for surveillance devices; although he found none, the man decided to conduct his activities as if the unpredictable Warlord himself was spying on them.

The girl watched him in dread as he quickly stripped off much of his clothing.

The big man selected the darkest corner of the quarters and pressed the whimpering waif into it.

"Now let's see what we have here!" Jasper grunted with exaggerated showmanship.

The girl pressed her eyes tightly closed for the upcoming onslaught.

"Don't worry," he whispered to the trembling little thing, "I won't hurt you."

Jasper continued his contrived attack, "I'm sure you're a fine play toy!"

She stared at the big man in growing disbelief.

"We've come to rescue you," the man murmured.

The girl nodded hopefully.

"AH! This will do nicely!" As he clattered boisterously from side to side, he continued his hushed assurances, "What's your name, sweetheart?"

"Dilma."

He groaned loudly like rutting beast. "Play along with me so your Master won't suspect anything."

She smiled mischievously to her liberator and screeched dramatically.

"Good," Jasper coaxed, "we're going to take you out of here Dilma, but I need you to do something very important before we leave." He banged loudly against the wall with his shoulders as he hunched protectively over the girl.

"OK," her big eyes glistened with hope.

• • •

The Ripple In Space-Time

"I must insist on at least fifty thousand Units for girl," Dimitri stated.

"Well, I suppose we will buy the perfectly acceptable child that we inspected in the Jupiter Colonies a few weeks ago for merely ten thousand then," Zmuda countered.

The leisurely bidding game progressed between the two men.

In the distance, the apparent carnal misdeeds of Jasper and the girl proceeded noisily.

"I don't want you to leave empty-handed," the Warlord chuckled, "perhaps I could let her go for forty."

An especially piercing scream filled the chamber.

Dimitri stared uneasily at the door.

"I doubt that he'll permanently damage the scamp," Zmuda reassured the man, "although she does seem quite frail."

The frightening crescendo of Jasper's thunderous bellows intertwined with the ragged adolescent shrieks of agony finally unnerved Dimitri. "I'll let her go for twenty."

"You have a deal, sir."
192

• • •

Jasper returned just as Zmuda was authorizing the payment for the slave girl. Both men secretly tapped their cheeks as a signal to the other that the plan was proceeding as expected.

"I trust you enjoyed yourself?" Zmuda teased.

"A little rough around the edges, but in time she'll improve," Jasper replied.

"Where is the brat?" Dimitri demanded.

"I told her to clean herself up and gather her possessions, assuming of course that an agreement would be reached."

The door slowly opened.

Dilma stood in absolute defeat at the portal, her face red and tear-stained, clutching a grimy bundle of meager belongings.

Jasper secretly marveled at the little actress's abilities.

"Gentlemen, do stop by again," the Warlord smiled.

The men bowed and left the chamber with the bedraggled slave girl in tow.

• • •

The Ripple In Space-Time

When the landing craft was well away from the giant moon of Saturn, Lieutenant Zmuda finally relaxed.

Jasper tousled the girl's hair as she studied her two stocky saviors in awe. "What did you get for us, sweetheart?"

Dilma grinned in triumph as she opened the little bundle.

The former parlormaid held up an antique hairbrush, three unwashed forks and a tightly wadded men's undergarment, all recently purloined from Dimitri Verhovnyi's bedchamber.

"Excellent," the Lieutenant complimented the young burglar; "we should have no problem extracting his DNA from these treasures."

30. Atonement

As Jasper coaxed the spacecraft into a high orbit around Titan, Zmuda prepared the freshly made assassin's weapon for Mixion as she waited in the airlock just outside the landing craft.

Dilma looked on with interest.

Mixion inattentively stroked the girl's sullied and tangled hair.

"Let me see your palms," the Lieutenant said.

The raven-skin woman displayed her hands. Thick and irregular calluses crossed high over both palms just below the fingers.

"Nicely done!" Zmuda commented.

"Thanks," Mixion said, "I found a knurled hand rail in the engine compartment. While you were away I spent hours twisting my hands around it."

Dilma stared at the woman's leathery hands with concern.

"It's OK, kitten," Mixion assured the child.

The former slave girl compared her own tiny white hands to Mixion's large ebony appendages.

Zmuda readied the syringe, "Do you have an explanation ready, in case it comes up?"

The woman nodded, "Rusty exercise equipment at the Europa Diplomatic Mission fitness center."

"Simple and unambiguous." The Lieutenant massaged the rough callus on her right palm for several seconds and carefully injected the thick milky fluid just under the skin to produce a long distended blister.

Mixion studied the bulging skin.

"Maximum lethality will last for about two days," Zmuda stared at her with a growing sense of dread. "If it takes that long to initiate the process, I suspect we'd all be done for anyway. Unfortunately it's not nearly as effective as I had hoped, but it will have to do on such short notice. The CRAMP's working on a more virulent strain called the y-pathogen."

Jasper joined the group at the landing craft, "Alright, I sent the message to the Palace and they're expecting 'Assistant Deputy Ambassador Mixion' in the next hour or so."

The woman climbed into the landing craft's pilot seat.

"Remember, you need to touch his bare skin as much as possible," Zmuda instructed her with more than a little remorse. Just before he closed the hatch, the Lieutenant added, "I'm sorry to say, my dear friend that, if need be, all four of us are considered expendable in this matter."

"Hopefully, it won't come to that," Mixion smiled nervously.

• • •

Just as Jasper and the Lieutenant had forewarned her, Mixion had undergone a careful search for weapons and several hours of lone isolation in a stark, cold cell.

When the sullen palace guard came for her, she clasped her hands together reverently and followed him. Using the sharp thumbnail on her left hand, the woman stealthily sawed back and forth across the swollen blister on her right palm.

As they reached the sturdy door of the Palace workroom, the skin split open and the opaque fluid trickled out.

Mixion feigned interest in the sentinel's droning lecture about etiquette as she steadily wrung her hands together to secretly spread the toxin that had been custom-made using the DNA from the personal items that Dilma had stolen.

She smiled disarmingly to the guard as he led her into the chamber.

"Oh Supreme Exalted Ruler of All Humanity," the sentry proclaimed, "Assistant Deputy Ambassador Mixion from the municipality of Free City has come to pay tribute to your excellence."

Dimitri Verhovnyi slowly rose from the desk chair.

Mixion bowed to the pompous tyrant.

"I must say," the Warlord began sourly, "that I'm rather disappointed that my first encounter with a representative of Free City only warranted a mere underling in the diplomatic corp."

"The Prime Minister sends his personal apologies, Oh Supreme Exalted Ruler."

A conceited little grin crossed Dimitri's face.

"The Free City government is of course most eager to establish a nonaggression pact with the unquestioned Master of All Humanity," Mixion nodded humbly. "Because the High Ambassador and his diplomatic entourage is still many weeks away, I was hastily sent from a minor posting in the Jupiter Colonies to convey the Prime Minster's most urgent aspirations for peace."

The Warlord appraised her worthiness for several seconds. "Please come in." Dimitri stared with an unnerving intensity at the young woman, "I don't recall ever laying eyes on such an unusually beautiful black woman."

"Why thank you!" Mixion placed her hand flirtatiously on Dimitri's forearm, "I've rarely received such a flattering compliment, and certainly never from such a high source." She slid her palm innocently back and forth over his skin, spreading the first of what she hoped would be at least three doses of the pathogen onto the man.

Dimitri was obviously aroused by the sensual trifling.

Mixion quickly shifted back to her diplomatic ruse; if need be to accomplish her deadly goal, she would return to the contrived seduction of the vile man. "I must apologize in advance, my Exalted Ruler; due to the urgent nature of this preliminary meeting and the complex gravitational difficulties imposed by Saturn, I will only be able to converse with you for a very short time before departing."

The Warlord frowned at the forewarning.

"To expedite the Prime Minister's goal," Mixion continued, "of a mutually beneficial agreement, I would like to ask you what terms shall the

High Ambassador propose to you in the upcoming meeting?"

The Warlord scowled at the sudden deflection away from his sexual interest in the woman. "I shall immediately require half interest in the Bank of Free City and payment of one half of all the tax proceeds collected by the municipal government. There of course will be many other requirements."

"I suspect that the Prime Minister will balk at that arrangement," she warned.

The man sighed obstinately, "I'm afraid the matter is nonnegotiable. After all, I have many weapons currently targeting the city that could rain down on the fools should they resist my demands."

Mixion strolled pensively around the chamber, apparently considering the difficult issue. "I understand," she finally said, "I shall apprise the Ambassador of your pressing wishes."

Dimitri leered at the petite woman.

She studied him carefully for a second opportunity to infect the repulsive man; frustratingly, none seemed obvious.

A wickedly manipulative thought crossed her

mind. She quickly weighed the various possible outcomes of the ploy and reluctantly concluded that despite her personal revulsion, she should proceed.

With her arms crossed in mock dismay, Mixion huffed, "I'm only twenty-five and I don't want to be stranded in the uneventful backwaters of the Jupiter Colonies for much longer." Her shoulders drooped. "I would dearly love a more prestigious assignment."

"My grand scheme for the future," the Warlord said with a twinkle of lechery in his eyes, "will be to have a full time staff of consulars from the fiefdoms, and of course Free City, here on Titan to attend to my decrees."

Mixion nodded with feigned interest; the vain man had greedily taken the bait that she had dangled before him.

She tipped her head playfully, "Perhaps you could suggest that the High Ambassador appoint me to a permanent position as Consular for Free City?"

"Perhaps."

Mixion slipped her hand into his as an apparent effort to seal the deal.

He squeezed her sweaty palm, "I will surely

require very intimate consultations with you if I decide that you are worthy of that distinguished post."

"Of course," she withdrew her hand with a satisfied grin. The second dose of the toxin had been delivered to the victim.

Mixion glanced out of the workroom window at the dusky red landscape of the fridge moon, "Sadly, as I mentioned earlier, I must leave Titan now and pilot my orbiting spacecraft back to a rendezvous with the High Ambassador's vessel."

Dimitri frowned at the prospect of losing her.

She gently stroked his cheek in mock sympathy, "I will see you again in several weeks when I accompany the diplomatic mission during the upcoming official meeting." The third portion of poison had been applied.

He cooed at the implied future liaison, "I look forward to it."

Mixion smiled disingenuously at the Warlord when she left him alone in the workroom; no matter what else happened to her in the ensuring minutes as she made her way back to the comparative safety of the orbiting ship, she had successfully carried out her part of the risky assassination effort.

31. News Item:
Verhovnyi culprit in Lab blast

Dateline: 25th of August, 2445; Free City, Earth

Anonymous sources in the Prime Minister's Office confirmed today that, as has been long suspected by most in Free City, Warlord Dimitri Verhovnyi of the Outer Reaches was indeed responsible for the destruction of the Ultra Energy Lab sixteen weeks ago.

The detested villain occupying the Titan Palace apparently engaged at least one pack of rapacious raiders to seize valuable and dangerous antimatter from the facility below the Sea of Crisis. It is believed that as a final act of vandalism, the thugs detonated the remaining stores of antimatter dooming the scientific institution and the scores of innocents who happened to be there.

Many in the fair city suspect that Verhovnyi's henchmen utilized the looted explosives to fabricate the warhead that obliterated Arusha.

Reporters have been unable to officially confirm the emerging details about the twin disasters: Both Chief Inspector Helga Bennet of the Inquisitor's Office and Principal Justice Tzai

The Ripple In Space-Time

Chong of the High Court refused to comment on the ongoing investigations.

With the current miserable state of affairs imposed upon us all by the self-proclaimed "Ruler of All Humanity," it seems unlikely that Dimitri Verhovnyi will ever be held accountable for the destruction of the Ultra Energy Laboratory and the murder of the 287 souls at the facility.

Sadly, most citizens of our fine city also doubt that the nine million residents of Arusha who perished recently on the Maasai Steppes at the hands of the tyrant will ever be avenged.

32. The long sought objectives

"This is the route that your sugar pie Benny took?" Lev stared accusingly at Keira as she piloted the *Seiran* slowly though the forsaken region of the interminable asteroid field.

The woman scowled at him, "What's that supposed to mean?"

"Well, you were hanging all over him in the bar. How do we know that he wasn't just toying with you?"

"He's only fifteen, you idiot!" she snarled. "I'm nearly old enough to be his mom."

Keira adjusted the craft's trajectory to avoid a mountain-sized boulder ahead. "That's how leads are developed."

Lev hastily retreated from his earlier disapproving tone. "Sorry."

She glanced at him, "Were you jealous of Benny?"

"I guess I was."

Keira smiled smugly at the revelation; their rocky romance had come full circle. "You know that I felt the same way when we went dancing and you dragged Desiree over to our table."

The woman glared at her heedless copilot, "You two were draped all over each other like dirty sheets on an unmade bed."

"Yeah; I messed up that night. I should have apologized sooner. Desiree is eccentric and enthralling," Lev rubbed his temple in dismay, "but I always seem to get into *way* too much trouble when I'm around her."

He shook his head remorsefully, "She's never been right for me."

Keira dodged around another obstacle. "Who *is* right for you?"

"You are."

After the ship had cleared the looming crag, she studied him for several seconds to appraise his sincerity.

He had a curious look of hope and remorse, she finally decided. "No more ignoring me when some fetching young thing walks by?"

"I'll try my best."

"And I'll remind you," Keira quipped in victory.

• • •

While his young crewmates slumbered together again in the berth, apparently putting an end to the weeks of sullen moodiness between them, Ryo inched the *Seiran* along through the floating rubble.

Keira was a much better pilot than he would ever be, the old Investigator had realized long ago, but the search had to continue when the woman required rest or other more sensual diversions.

In the endless tedium of grays and blacks that was the Asteroid Belt, an unusual gleamer caught his eye. Ryo concentrated on the distant anomaly. After several seconds of squinting to no avail, he was nearly ready to give up on the shiny phantasm.

There!

Far off in the chaotic jumble of jostling worldlets, a tiny speck blinked at him with a silvery flash.

Ryo checked the wide scan radar. Nearly fifty kilometers away a colossal spacecraft sat stranded amongst the stony behemoths.

He quickly shutdown the radar and engaged the anti-detection system.

"LEV! KEIRA! I've found something!"

The Ripple In Space-Time

The drowsy duo rattled clumsily down the passageway.

Keira straightened her ruffled nightshirt and Lev stared dumbly at the control panel.

Ryo searched for the elusive vessel with the ancient telescope, "I see it! I'm sure it's the *Xenon Lightning*."

"Do you see the *Butin Belle*?" Lev asked hopefully.

"No; but I'm not surprised, the *Belle* is tiny compared to the tanker."

He handed the spyglass to the young man.

"I'll be right back," Keira frowned, "I'm going to check on something." She left the men in the cockpit and floated back to the gravitational survey compartment.

Lev set the old instrument aside, "All I could see was the *Lightning*."

"The weird antimatter doesn't seem to be there!" Keira called to the men.

"I don't think that the *Lightning* is moving enough for the scanner to detect the stuff," Lev said with a hint of doubt.

208

The woman returned to the cockpit.

"I suspect that it will take days of delicate stalking," Ryo concluded as he watched for the periodic glint of the distant ship, "but let's see if we can creep up on that beast undetected."

• • •

It had indeed taken days, as the old Investigator had predicted, for the *Seiran* to sneak up on the hijacked tanker.

The trio had spent hours shortly after the discovery of the *Lightning* painstakingly plotting an elaborate and stealthy course to intercept the marooned vessel. Lev had suggested a zigzag route that took advantage of the cover offered by the many asteroids that littered the gulf between the ships. Keira recommended that the *Seiran's* maneuvering engines should only be engaged when the craft was shielded behind the floating debris. The interceptor would then slowly drift to the next rock a few kilometers away and begin the drawn out process again.

Ryo had warned his crewmates to be ready for a quick chase should the pirates detect the creeping craft.

Now the huge *Xenon Lightning* loomed about a kilometer ahead.

"I'm still not picking up anything on the gravitational scanner," Lev reported. "Well, other than the tanker and the usual clatter of the surrounding rubble."

As the *Seiran* glided towards the derelict tanker, Ryo and Keira studied the monster from the darkened cockpit. With the exception of a few feeble marker lights, the vessel showed no signs of life.

Keira slowly shook her head, "Where is the *Butin Belle*?"

• • •

"Why did we abandon my friends?" Jana snapped at Bosco when he finally opened the hatch to the chamber.

For nearly a day she'd been locked away again in the tiny cell onboard the *Butin Belle*. To her great dread, Jana had watched the *Lightning* slowly recede though the porthole. Although she was worried about her slave companions still onboard the tanker, Jana was especially anxious to know about the status of the three booby-trapped weapons that they had constructed for their captors.

The big First Mate laughed, "Well, it's nice to see you too, sweetheart." He motioned towards the door.

She took a deep breath and relaxed; Jana was most certainly still a prisoner, if she hoped to discover anything about the abrupt change she would need to seem cooperative.

"Sorry Boz, I'm really hungry." Jana followed him down the corridor.

He glanced back at her; "I'll get you some chow in a few hours."

"Thanks." She tugged on his sleeve, "Can I check over the devices? I'd like to make sure that the containment bubbles haven't degraded."

The gruff marauder considered her request for several seconds, "Well, since I'd prefer not to be blown halfway to hell by a faulty bomb, I guess we could take a few minutes to examine the little beasties."

Jana nodded, "It would be a good idea."

They diverted into a large side compartment. In the center of the room, clamped firmly into launching fixtures, sat the three small weapons.

The pirate pointed to the munitions, "Knock yourself out, Doc."

Jana pried open the first device, casually maneuvering around to block Boz's view of the object. With a smooth and well-practiced motion, she secretly reset the doomsday timer and resealed the cover, "This one looks OK. Why did we leave the *Lightning*?"

He tepidly watched her float to the second sphere, "Our employer, who still owes us a great deal of money, gave up the ghost a few days ago."

She nonchalantly restarted the second timer, "Really? That's sad."

"He was a friggin' weasel and would have tried to cheat us out of our due."

Jana stopped at the third bomb and studied the man, "What's to become of this enterprise that you and the Captain have been engaged in for so long?"

"We're tending to that right now," Boz smiled ominously. "You and the *Lightning* will eventually be ransomed. The men will be sold off for slave work in a few months to a mine somewhere."

"I suspect my son would be interested in getting me back alive." She swiveled around and reset the third device, "What about these weapons?"

"The three little gems will be used to blackmail the simpletons on Earth."

212

33. News item: Death of the despot?

Dateline: 1st of September, 2445; Free City University, Free City, Earth

"Amazing, if true!" crowed one ecstatic revealer during the wild impromptu celebration late last night near the War Atrocities Monument in Roscommon Park.

Several hundred students mainly from the University's Department of Advanced Applied Molecular Biology gathered at the normally somber monument around midnight when sketchy tidbits regarding the death of Dimitri Verhovnyi first materialized. Although no source, reliable or otherwise, could be sniffed out to verify what many believe is merely wishful thinking, the rumors have persisted.

University officials remain perplexed by what many students now claim is true. Several instructors in the School of Psychology attribute the hearsay to Enlightenment Crusade crackpots.

The prevailing buzz involves the dictator falling ill shortly after an unexpected visitor claiming to be an envoy from our fair city departed from the Titan Palace. Accounts remain fuzzy, but many jubilant students maintain that after Verhovnyi became comatose, he was bludgeoned to death by palace slaves who then hung their despised master alongside his long-dead father on the surface of the icy moon.

This morning the Prime Minister's Office dismissed the speculation as ludicrous, pointedly noted that the city's official diplomatic delegation is in route to Titan and is still more than sixty days away from the Warlord's palace.

34. Advanced Mission Completed

"She's a lovely child," Mixion commented to the men.

It had taken nearly a week of intermittent scrubbing to finally remove the many layers of dirt that had begrimed the girl; recently outfitted in Mixion's spare flight suit, Dilma finally resembled a conventional eleven-year-old.

The former slave had taken to tidying up the crowded spacecraft; perhaps as a familiar diversion during the interminable return to Earth.

Jasper peered over the interface display and studied the purposeful youngster as she retrieved wayward objects floating about the cabin, "I imagine that someday she'll make an excellent espionage agent."

The girl smiled sweetly to the doting adults.

Zmuda chuckled at the suggestion, "She certainly can act the part and her abilities to nab unattended valuables is already legendary."

In the many days since they had departed from the Titan Palace, the former parlormaid had managed to accumulate a huge and very carefully hidden trove of unguarded treasures.

Whenever a toothbrush or control knob went missing, the adults would spend hours playfully coaxing their beloved ragamuffin into returning the pilfered item.

"What's going to become of her when we return to Free City?" the woman asked.

Zmuda brooded over the nettlesome matter. "I don't know."

• • •

The Lieutenant studied the classified message from Earth with interest.

Back in Free City, his associates in the CRAMP were already developing an intricate new effort to destabilize the Fiefdom of IndoPacifica. The elderly and enfeebled Warlord of the scattered realm would certainly be a much easier target than Dimitri Verhovnyi.

The CRAMP had organized a robust subversive movement in New Rome since the city had become the de facto capital of EurAfrica following the destruction of Arusha and the death of Daniel Kufuzu. In progressively larger and louder demonstrations around the city, the citizens were making it clear that they would not tolerate a return to the corrupt feudal system of the past.

New Roman authorities were slowly capitulating to the inevitable change.

Zmuda grinned with proud satisfaction when he read that hundreds of Enlightenment Crusaders from Free City University had converged on New Rome to lend their support to the local revolutionaries. For the first time in nearly two centuries, many more people were flooding out of Free City then were clamoring to get in.

Dr. Suzuki had taken over his half dozen classes in the Department of Advanced Applied Molecular Biology. Although the grades of his students had dipped slightly since his abrupt departure, Zmuda was satisfied that the fledgling instructor had sufficiently motivated his eager young charges.

The tireless Suzuki had also cloned several new members of the CRAMP from the secret old database that Zmuda had used earlier to produce Jasper and Mixion. When the Lieutenant and his cohorts eventually returned to the University in many months, there would be plenty of untraceable agents that the CRAMP could deploy.

But the most startling news for the clandestine organization was the secret vow of support from the Free City Prime Minister. A great deal of money had been surreptitiously diverted from other projects to fund the CRAMP for the next few years.

Perhaps now, Zmuda speculated, with the first wobbly steps away from the tyranny and subjugation of the past, the CRAMP would achieve its goal of allowing all humans to live freely once more.

• • •

It was the middle of the night, shipboard time; although Zmuda noticed with some amusement that the craft's control panel indicated that it was midmorning Universal Time. He had carefully calculated the optimum hour to transmit this particular communiqué, taking into account the relative locations of the two vessels, the sleeping patterns of his crewmates and the likelihood that the recipient would be available to respond.

Thankfully, due to the dwindling amount of propellent remaining after the mad dash to Titan, the return speed of his spacecraft was now ridiculously slow and he would be able to enjoy a long conversation before he slipped out of range.

The Lieutenant entered the connection information and the vessel's communication system began the methodical automated search through the profusion of asteroids far below.

After nearly an hour of patient waiting, the contact acknowledgment light flashed.

He had found his compatriot.

"Ryo Trop, Zmuda here! We've arching over your location on the way back to Earth."

"Lieutenant! I noticed that the encryption is 'on;' is this another Top Secret message?"

"No," he chortled, "only medium secret. I don't want any eavesdroppers in the Belt to discover my dual identities."

"Fair enough."

"We were quite successful with our effort on Titan. The x-pathogen worked acceptably well, although I'll have to improve the virility and simplify the delivery system," Zmuda reported.

"Are the Outer Reaches Warlord-free?"

"Yes," the Lieutenant said with great satisfaction. "We deployed a tiny satellite to snoop on Titan before we left. Evidently the palace slaves finished off Dimitri on his deathbed. I have a spectacular surveillance photo of his corpse dangling alongside his father's on the moon's surface. If necessary, the CRAMP will use the image to allay fears of future attacks by the lunatic."

"That's great news. Can I share it with my crew?"

"Please do. How is your quest for the pirates and the missing munitions?"

"Well," Ryo vacillated, "it's not working out as well as your recent effort."

Zmuda frowned, "My condolences. Bring me up to date."

"We dug up a lucky tip in a bar on one of the nearby asteroids about a marooned supertanker."

"*The Xenon Lightning*?" the Lieutenant interrupted.

"Yes, how did you guess?"

"One of my CRAMP cronies discovered a morsel about a group of fairly inept raiders called the Kuiper Belt Shipjacks. Someone had paid them an absurd amount of money to commandeer the unladened vessel. We wondered over a few beers why anyone would hijack an empty tanker when a fully loaded one would be worth trillions more."

"We're guessing that it was some sort of hideout. Unfortunately the pirates along with the all-important antimatter have slipped away."

"Are you back to sniffing around on a cold trail?"

"Luckily no. We're tracking them using a gravitational distortion that the strange stuff onboard the ship produces but with all of the clatter caused by the asteroids it is quite a challenge."

Zmuda winced; with the antimatter still at large, continuing blackmail was inevitable. "I wish you the greatest of luck in your search."

"We certainly need it right now," Ryo groaned.

"In a more minor matter, during our shindig at the Titan Palace we acquired a new crew member. She's an adolescent former slave girl and an exceptionally wonderful child. I'd love to find an especially attentive guardian for her when we return to Free City."

"Interesting."

"Do you know of anyone who might be up to the task?" Zmuda wondered.

"Perhaps," Ryo replied after a protracted silence.

35. The payoff

"See?" Lev said.

Ryo tilted his head and tried to make sense of the speckled image on the gravitational scanner. "I'm really not very good at this sort of thing."

Lev traced his finger over the screen, "This is the stolen antimatter. I'm guessing that the pirates are now moving fast enough that we can detect the heavy stuff that they stole from the lunar lab."

"Any idea where they are?"

Lev made some calculations, "About twenty kilometers away and trudging along at five kilometers per hour towards the edge of the Asteroid Belt."

"Alright; I'd like to stop them before they reach open space. Go up to the cockpit and help Keira track them down."

• • •

Keira nudged the *Seiran* gently over a tumbling asteroid.

"There they are!" Lev pointed to the left. "The

Belle is much bigger than I imagined," he noted with dismay.

The hijacked Ore Runner dwarfed the Interceptor that was sent to overtake it.

Ryo studied the distant vessel, "The *Butin Belle* is unarmed and the pirates don't know that we're stalking them."

Keira gloated, "We've got quite an arsenal of weapons, if push comes to shove."

"I guess that will all help," Lev turned to his crewmates in bewilderment. "How exactly are we going to get them to stop?"

The old Investigator stared at the Liaison Officer turned hotshot spacecraft pilot in sudden consternation.

Keira shook her head.

"I have no idea," Ryo groaned.

• • •

For hours Keira had cautiously skirted in a wide arc around the slow moving Ore Runner, now they were dead ahead of the big vessel cloaked by a cloud of floating rubble that had undoubtedly been a hefty asteroid at some point in the past.

"Pull up and switch off the anti-detection system," Ryo said.

Keira complied.

For several tense minutes, the *Belle* continued towards the little craft.

Ryo switched on the ship to ship radio, "The is Inspector Trop of the Free City Inquisitor's Office, stop and prepare to be boarded."

"I'm afraid not Inspector."

"Then we will open fire."

"With what?"

Ryo pointed to Keira and she blasted a small asteroid several hundred meters to the side of the *Butin Belle*, sending a glowing shower of incandescent gravel in all directions.

The maneuvering thrusters on the big ship reluctantly fired and the Ore Runner came to a halt.

A gruff voice boomed over the radio in the *Seiran*, "We seem to have a stand off, Inspector."

Ryo pondered the situation for many minutes.

"We have reliable information that you are holding a hostage and are in possession of stolen property."

"Yes we are!" snorted the unseen outlaw. "We have one Doctor Jana Fesai, formerly a resident of the Ultra Energy Lab on the Sea of Crisis. You can get her back with a suitable payment."

"Dr. Fesai was killed," Ryo signaled to his confused shipmates that his comment to the pirates was a ruse.

"Say something to the nice Inspector, sweetie," the pirate prompted.

"Ah," a hoarse woman uttered, "I'm...Jana Fesai."

"I have the Doctor's dossier right here," Ryo continued, "let's see if the details match up. The Doctor has a townhouse in Free City; on what street is it located?"

The woman's shaky voice strengthened, "Breton Street."

Lev's head slowly bobbed as he listened to the familiar sound.

"Ms Fesai has a pet at that house. What type of animal is it and what is its name?"

"Iridium!" the radio reverberated. "My cat's name is Iridium. He lives with my son, Lev on Breton Street in the Old Town District of Free City!"

Lev pressed his hands to his face and quietly whimpered with relief. Touchingly, Ryo watched as Keira wrapped her arms protectively around the tearful man.

"Alright; I'm satisfied," the Investigator said. "We'd like to get her back."

"One million Units," the outlaw snorted defiantly.

Ryo rolled his eyes, "It's a person you're ransoming, not a hijacked freighter."

The pirate laughed, "Just checking to see if you're paying attention, Inspector. We'll let her go for five hundred thousand."

"No deal," Ryo bluffed.

Lev stared at the old Investigator in shock.

He signaled to the young man to remain quiet.

"Well I guess we'll kill her then."

Ryo smiled wryly, now the pirates were bluffing, "Everyone thinks she dead already."
226

The trio on board the *Seiran* could hear the outlaws arguing about what to do next.

"Alright," the pirate continued, "make an offer."

"Ten thousand," Ryo quickly bid.

"Fifty!" the raider shouted back.

"Fifteen."

"Twenty five."

Ryo nodded, "We'll pay twenty five thousand, but I want a hand to hand exchange to insure there's no double-crossing."

"Deal."

Lev was visibly relieved.

"Mr. Trop," the pirate continued, "you may dock with and board our fine ship to take possession of Dr. Fesai. Kindly bring along a payment interface showing a deposit of twenty five thousand Units made to Gristle's Raiders."

"No weapons," Ryo countered.

"Fair enough."

• • •

While Keira brought the *Seiran* along side the much larger ship and gently prodded the craft towards the docking port, she listened to the men as they engaged in some sort of secretive planning.

"Here," Lev pointed to the screen as Ryo looked on with interest, "and here."

"And that will achieve the desired effect?" the old Investigator asked.

"It should, but it'll take a little while."

Ryo ruminated on the risky plan before answering, "OK; do it then."

• • •

"Bosco Kremerling?" Ryo inquired of the burly man who met him and Keira at the docking hatch.

"Call me Boz," the First Mate said absently. "We don't often have visitors," he chuckled sarcastically, "please excuse the untidiness."

Ryo warily appraised the big man.

The pirate studied Keira with interest. "I'll trade you this one for the old hag straight away," he sneered.

228

Keira growled at the man.

"And feisty, no less," the First Mate remarked.

Ryo glared at the pirate, "The original deal only."

"It's your money."

They followed Boz down a long passageway to the control room of the ship. There, loosely strapped to a communication panel, was a haggard middle-aged woman. At last, they had located the long missing scientist.

A wiry man watched the new arrivals with interest, "Welcome to the *Butin Belle*, I am Captain Olin Gristle."

"Captain," Ryo nodded tepidly. "I'm Inspector Trop and this is my associate, Liaison Officer Norton."

Gristle held out his hand, "The money please."

Keira handed a payment interface to the Captain.

Gristle entered several numbers and smiled, "Excellent; I see that the payment has been properly credited."

The First Mate released the hostage and she swiftly joined her liberators.

"Gentleman," Ryo scowled at the fugitives, "I'm arresting you under the authority of the Free City High Court and the Warlord Syndicate."

The Captain laughed.

Boz smirked, "Well you see Inspector Trop, we don't plan to go with you now that we've extracted the ransom for the old crone."

The two groups scrutinized each other suspiciously.

When the tension of the stand off finally got the better of her, Keira lunged at the burly First Mate but he easily deflected her. The big man reached behind the communications panel and produced a potent looking side arm and a long glinting dagger.

"You have two choices," Boz waved the weapons ominously, "get the hell off the ship or die right here like the stupid fools that you are."

Ryo spun around and pushed the women towards the docking hatch. "LET'S GET OUT OF HERE!"

36. Reunion

"GET IN!" Lev quickly pulled his mother and the boarding party through the docking hatch.

Keira slammed the door closed.

A disturbing low-level vibration rattled through the ship.

"DID YOU DO IT?" Ryo shouted to the young man.

"YES!"

The *Seiran* shuddered painfully as the pirates engaged the huge engine of the *Butin Belle*.

Ryo hammered the 'Emergency Docking Disengage' button and the predacious Interceptor grudgingly unleashed the much larger Ore Runner.

The rapidly building thrust of the escaping vessel violently battered the patrol craft as it whipped past.

From the radio in the cockpit, the raucous cackling of the escaping criminals echoed though the *Seiran*.

The Ripple In Space-Time

When the brutal pummeling finally subsided,
Lev embraced his recently liberated mother. "I
knew you weren't dead," he whispered.

Jana stared at him with misty eyes, "I almost was
more than once."

Keira shook her head in dismay, "I can't believe
that they got away with the antimatter."

Still panting from the panicky escape, Ryo
grinned knowingly at Lev, "They'll never collect
on the ransom."

"How can you be sure?" Keira asked.

Lev chuckled, "While you and Ryo were
onboard the pirate's ship, I sent a surreptitious
command signal to the *Belle*."

Jana tilted her head in confusion.

"What good did that do?" Keira asked in
annoyance. "They're still at large."

He kissed her forehead, "I permanently jammed
the engine to maximum output and locked out
the maneuvering and override controls."

Both of the women slowly nodded as they
grasped the implications of the tampering.

Keira smiled, "They're stuck going straight ahead at full blast?"

"Until they eventually run out of propellant," Ryo snorted.

Lev laughed as he wrapped an arm around Keira, "The *Belle* will coast forever through deep space after that, although without an energy source, I suspect that the life support systems will give out in a week or two."

"I can't believe that you come halfway across the Solar System to get me," Jana stared her son.

Lev beamed at the attention.

Ryo started down the passageway towards the cockpit, "Let's see if we can figure out where the doomed raiders are headed."

"So you two are an item?" Jana asked the Liaison Officer as they followed the old Investigator.

"Yeah, I guess we are," Keira blushed.

Lev nodded tentatively, "We got off to a shaky start, but we're doing pretty well now."

Keira kissed his cheek, "I think we were both hopelessly smitten with each other at different times. It just took us a long time to finally get past the superficial exteriors and really appreciate each other."

Lev smiled.

"I suspect that you'll both do well together." Jana noted. "I can't wait to get back to Free City," she squeezed through the corridor with the others, "I'd just love to have a hot bath, a really big meal and a chance to reread *Macbeth*."

"*Macbeth*?" Lev asked.

"Anything but *A Midsummer Night's Dream*," Jana groaned.

"I thought that was your favorite Shakespearian play?"

"It *was*."

The group crowded into the cockpit.

"When we return," Ryo intoned, "I plan to exercise my option for an early retirement."

"Retire?" Keira stared at him in disbelief. "What on earth are you going to do with all of that free time?"

"There's a little girl that I heard about recently who'll need an especially steady hand to guide her into adulthood," Ryo said with a strange faraway look in his eyes. "Perhaps I'll take on that challenge."

The weary foursome watched from the cockpit windows as the *Butin Belle* streaked past the ragged edge of the Asteroid Belt. After many minutes, all that could be seen of escaping fugitives was the sinister violet-blue exhaust from the burly ion engine.

"What about the others still locked away on the *Lightning*?" Jana asked Ryo. "I don't think that we could possibly fit them into this ship."

"Not to worry," he assured her, "a couple of Syndicate Tugs are on the way from Vesta to salvage the tanker and rescue the occupants."

While the disdainful taunts of the escaping pirates filled the cramped cockpit, each of the four brooding shipmates of the overcrowded *Seiran* considered the doleful rubble field and the vast celestial vista beyond.

"We weren't able to haul the criminals back to Free City to stand trail, but thankfully no one will be troubled by those marauders again," Ryo assured the others.

Jana smiled wickedly; with no one onboard the *Butin Belle* to reset the doomsday timers on the three devices, the fate of the pirates would be settled in less than two days.

"They'll get what they deserve," Jana whispered spitefully as she studied the far-off purplish streak from the engine exhaust.

37. The old African

Far out in the night darkened Maasai steppes,
sheltered from the lingering radiation by the
northern flanks of Mount Meru, the ancient
African man set aside the gazelle thigh that he
had been feasting upon for most of the evening.

The breeze smelled of dung and fresh grass, a
favorable sign of many more successful hunts to
come.

Just before sundown he had killed a juvenile
gazelle with the broad-tipped steel spear that had
been passed down for many generations in his
family.

The old Maasai hunter had severed his favorite
parts from the warm carcass after thanking the
animal for giving its life to feed him.

He left the remains to the lions that he had seen
earlier on the far edge of the herd. They too
would surely thank the young gazelle for filling
their bellies.

A mzungu doctor had visited his little hut nearly
a week ago and warned him that the great fire
that had seared away Arusha months ago had
contaminated the animals that now grazed on the

steppes. But he didn't care. He would die when he died; until then he would live as hundreds of generations had done before him, by their skill at hunting on the broad African plains.

The campfire had dwindled to a shimmering mound of red embers. Soon he would return to his hut to sleep.

The canopy of stars above him shimmered as well. In the distance a lion roared, perhaps calling to its pride or warning away the hyenas that bedeviled the big cats at every opportunity.

Amongst the crowd of stars, he noticed a tiny blue one grow suddenly much brighter. Wispy violet flares stretched out from the celestial visitor as it moved slowly across the sky.

He watched for many minutes until the unusual comet gradually faded.

The old man smiled to himself, it was surely another favorable omen for the creatures of the Maasai steppes.

Appendix

List of characters

In order of appearance:

Inspector Second Class Ryo Trop Mr. Trop is currently employed as an Investigator for the Free City Inquisitor's Office. He is a divorcee, has no children and is a long time resident of Free City. The 54 year-old is a sequential clone of his late father Ezo Trop.

Lev Fesai The 28 year-old only child of the well-respected Professor and Researcher Dr. Jana Fesai has been halfheartedly pursuing a Doctorate Degree in Physics at Free City University. Mr. Fesai has been a longtime member of the mildly subversive movement called the Enlightenment Crusade. He currently resides at his mother's townhouse on Breton Street in the Old Town District of Free City.

Chief Inspector Helga Bennet The 68 year-old hard-nosed and cynical head of the Free City Inquisitor's Office rarely sleeps as she directs the many ongoing investigations at the renowned agency.

Mining Guild Appraiser Thacker Tough, corrupt and immoral, Thacker frequents sleazy nightspots in Free City and elsewhere when he is not extracting "fees" from both legitimate and illicit mining operations for the Guild.

Dr. Jana Fesai Ph.D. Born in Buenos Aires on August 23, 2393, Dr. Fesai is currently the Chief Researcher at the Lunar Ultra Energy Research Laboratory on the plains of the Sea of Crisis. The 51 year-old Nobel Prizing winning Physicist has taught for many years at Free City University. She is unmarried and has an adult son.

First Mate Bosco Kremerling Rowdy and often foolhardy, the 48 year-old pirate has spent many years in the Outer Reaches Penitentiary. Kremerling was imprisoned when he was caught at the Kuiper Belt Station with illegally obtained Xenon most likely looted from the Kuiper Belt Gas Refinement Facility. Often seen in the company of Olin Gristle, his current location is unknown.

Captain Olin Gristle Thought to be about 42 years old, little else is known about the pirate Captain who is currently believed to be involved in the recent hijacking of the Ore Runner Class Midget space freighter *Butin Belle*.

Dimitri Verhovnyi, the Supreme Imperial Warlord of the Outer Reaches The especially violent 46 year-old half brother of Daniel Kufuzu became a Warlord when he killed his father to assume control over the vast and thinly populated Outer Reaches which extends from Saturn to the fringes of deep space. Producing great wealth from bribery, mining, slavery, and most recently the construction of the Kuiper Gas Refinement Facility, Dimitri Verhovnyi rules from his palace on Titan, the huge moon of Saturn.

Desiree MacFarland This quirky 24 year-old art student at Free City University is a long time member of the Enlightenment Crusade. She lived with Lev Fesai for nearly two years at his townhouse on Breton Street.

Sabra MacFarland Nineteen years old and a part-time student at Free City University, Sabra is Desiree's younger sister. Idealistic and naive, she often emulates the antics of her idolized older sister.

Cyndi Currently one of the many housemates of Lev Fesai.

Deputy Assistant Liaison Agent Norton The 26 year-old spent several years living in the fiefdoms as one of the several chidden of Jen and Bill Norton while the family searched for merchandise for their well-known Free City business "Leitrim Importers." This early experience abroad provided Agent Norton with invaluable knowledge of the people and conventions in the fiefdoms. Agent Norton is considered an especially promising new addition to the Free City Fiefdom Liaison Office.

Professor Malcolm Evans/ Lieutenant Zmuda
Very few know of this 43 year-old's dual
personas. As Lieutenant Zmuda he is currently
the leader of the super-secret CRAMP
Operation, a covert organization centered at Free
City University and dedicated to the overthrow
of the Warlords and the return of freedom to the
citizens of the fiefdoms. As Professor Malcolm
Evans he is a beloved instructor in the
Department of Advanced Applied Molecular
Biology and an occasional advisor for the
Enlightenment Crusade.

**Daniel Kufuzu, the Exalted Warlord of
EurAfrica** Although thoroughly corrupt and
manipulative, the EurAfrican Warlord is
considered by many to be the least tyrannical of
the seven Warlords that rule most of humanity.
The 62 year-old oversees the wealthiest and most
populated of the seven fiefdoms from his opulent
palace in huge capital city of Arusha in East
Africa.

Dr. Carla Stuhr The tall, dark haired 25 year-
old is a Junior Researcher Astronomer for the
Solar System Gravitational Anomalies Project at
Free City University. Although currently single,
Dr. Stuhr briefly lived on Breton Street with Lev
Fesai.

The Spanish teenager The nearly 18 year-old
young man from Madrid has been backpacking
across Europe and Africa. His goal is to scale at

least three of Africa's highest peaks before he turns 19.

The old African It is entirely unclear as whether this is two different people or merely one.

Mixion Fahmi A mysterious sequential clone of a long dead petite Australian Aboriginal woman from the mid Twenty-first century, Mixion was secretly produced by Lieutenant Zmuda using an unusual new procedure in the Advanced Biology lab at Free City University. She has been working since then as an agent for the CRAMP.

Jasper Pomeroy Originally from Blackall, Queensland. Like Mixion, Jasper is a clone of a long dead Australian. Big, burly and redheaded; Jasper was produced by Lieutenant Zmuda to act as an untraceable agent for the CRAMP.

Dilma The tremulous eleven-year-old slave girl is currently a parlormaid at the Titan Palace for Warlord Dimitri Verhovnyi of the Outer Reaches. It seems likely that she will be sold into sex slavery in the coming years.

Benny With his brothers, fifteen-year-old Benny secretly mines Rock 853111, a small asteroid near Lutetia in the Main Asteroid Belt. He frequently delivers ore to the Lutetia Asteroid Mining Facility.

The spacecraft:

Butin Belle Built at the Vesta Shipworks in 2429, the comparatively small, fast and highly maneuverable Ore-Runner Class midget space freighter was used by illicit miners in the Main Asteroid Belt for many years to evade Mining Guild inspectors. More recently the small freighter has been used by Celestial Delivery Systems as a quick transporter between Mars and the Kuiper Belt Station in the Outer Reaches.

Xenon Lightning 54 Plying the Solar System for the past four years, the immense robotic gas supertanker is the first of five vessels to be built to transport valuable Xenon gas from the huge Kuiper Gas Refinement Facility in the Outer Reaches to the inner Solar System. The *Xenon Lightning 54* is currently valued at an astonishing 3.5 trillion Standard Units.

Seiran The newest of more than a dozen long-duration patrol craft used primarily by Free City Law enforcement personal. The *Seiran* can easily accommodate up to six people for more than a year. The heavily armed and very maneuverable Interceptor Class ship can reach speeds of up to 45 Astronomical Units per year. The *Seiran* is currently registered to the Free City Inquisitor's Office and stationed in Low Earth Orbit.

"Fast prototype interceptor" Little is known about this secret, diminutive and unnamed experimental four-seater spacecraft. It is equipped with a tiny landing craft suitable for two passengers. The highly innovative vessel was produced by Free City engineers for the Municipal Government and its speed is rumored to exceed 75 Astronomical Units per year. It has been recently speculated that the craft is housed in a top-secret black ops hanger at the Ballyshannon Space Port.

About the book:

During the warm and sleepy mid-summer's days of 2010, I had a few gossamer ideas for a new science fiction tale floating around in my head.

I now suspect that these bits and pieces came to me at that particular time mainly as an intriguing distraction to draw my attention away from the more pressing and daunting task of beginning my third novel, the soft science fiction piece entitled *Xea In The Library*.

Xea is the sequel to my first work, the post-apocalyptic mystery called *Floyd 5.136*.

In one of those wonderful little moments of inspiration that led to much larger things, an irresistible title came to me while taking a long, hot shower: *The Ripple In Space-Time*.

I'd been considering the intriguing notion of 'Space-Time,' Albert Einstein's speculation that space and time are inextricability linked together as the four dimension, after enjoying Isaac Asimov's nonfiction work *Atom: A Journey Across the Subatomic Cosmos*, CalTech's fantastic *Mechanical Universe* video lectures and Carl Sagan's seminal series Cos*mos*.

The title fused together with a first chapter during a burst of nervous energy on the afternoon of August 12th.

For months I had been playing around with the idea of alternating viewpoints in a novel and I decided to write chapter 1 in the dry, formal style of a newspaper obituary. Where the novel would go from there, I had no idea at the time.

With *Xea In The Library* looming, I set *The Ripple* aside.

Almost exactly 6 months later, I returned to *The Ripple In Space-Time*.

Of all of my four novels to date, I had the most fun writing this sometimes brutal, sometimes poignant and often quite tongue-in-check tale.

The Ripple In Space-Time is one of a large group of novels that I've written or plan to pen soon that fit into a consistent history that stretches from the present to more than eighteen thousand years into the future. Several of the novels are consecutive and are best enjoyed and understood if read as such. These are part of the MAC series: currently *Floyd 5.136, Xea in the Library* and *Beyond the Habitable Limit* with others likely to follow.

The Ripple In Space-Time is not part of the MAC series but refers to much of the same history. Enjoy it separately or at any point while reading the MAC series.

All three of my editors expressed a desire to read at least one more tale involving the characters and settings in *The Ripple In Space-Time*.

Perhaps Inspector Ryo Trop and the others will return.

Enjoy,

S F Chapman, July 2011.

If you enjoyed *The Ripple in Space-Time* by
S F Chapman you might also like the literary fiction
novella *I'm here to help*.

I'm here to help

A NOVEL BY
S F CHAPMAN

It had all seemed so right at the time, Sharon realized with
a shudder.

Long ago she had made a collection of tiny and innocent
decisions that had precipitated a most profound and
unpredictable outcome.

Minutes ago her seventeen-year-old daughter, Renita had
stumbled upon the subtle inconsistencies of her birth while
completing some college applications. Now she waited
reproachfully for Sharon to explain the discrepancies.

It was clearly the time; Sharon brooded uneasily, when she
would have to finally disclose to her daughter both the
laudable good deeds and the lamentable oversights that
had led them to the current situation.

S F Chapman's exciting new novel
On The Back of The Beast
will be available in 2013.

Everyone knew it was coming but no one was sure just when it would happen.

It had been over a hundred years since the last big one had decimated the San Francisco Bay Area and another massive tremor was long overdue. The slumbering beast that is the Hayward Fault finally awoke on an ordinary October morning, catching the 7 million people of Bay Area by surprise as they tended to their routine affairs.

Will seventeen-year-old Kayla Hendley, airline pilot Burt Weaver, precocious second grader Gwen Mills and many others live through the convolutions of the angry earth?

The lives of ordinary people will be forever changed by the colossal natural disaster that is *The Beast*.

www.ingramcontent.com/pod-product-compliance
Lightning Source LLC
Chambersburg PA
CBHW070339260626
47160CB00003B/1092